Slaughterhouse-Five

OR

THE CHILDREN'S CRUSADE

Slaughterhouse-Five

OR

THE CHILDREN'S CRUSADE

A DUTY-DANCE WITH DEATH

BY

Kurt Vonnegut, Jr.

A FOURTH-GENERATION GERMAN-AMERICAN
NOW LIVING IN EASY CIRCUMSTANCES
ON CAPE COD
[AND SMOKING TOO MUCH],
WHO, AS AN AMERICAN INFANTRY SCOUT
HORS DE COMBAT,
AS A PRISONER OF WAR,
WITNESSED THE FIRE-BOMBING
OF DRESDEN, GERMANY,
"THE FLORENCE OF THE ELBE,"
A LONG TIME AGO,
AND SURVIVED TO TELL THE TALE.
THIS IS A NOVEL
SOMEWHAT IN THE TELEGRAPHIC SCHIZOPHRENIC
MANNER OF TALES
OF THE PLANET TRALFAMADORE,
WHERE THE FLYING SAUCERS
COME FROM.
PEACE.

A DELTA BOOK

For
Mary O'Hare
and
Gerhard Müller

A DELTA BOOK

Published by

Dell Publishing Co., Inc.
750 Third Avenue, New York, N.Y. 10017

Delta ® TM 755118, Dell Publishing Co., Inc.
Reprinted by arrangement with
Delacorte Press, A Seymour Lawrence Book, New York, New York
Manufactured in the United States of America
Seventh Printing

Grateful acknowledgment is made for permission to reprint the following material:

"The Waking": copyright 1953 by Theodore Roethke from THE COLLECTED POEMS OF THEODORE ROETHKE. Reprinted by permission of Doubleday & Company, Inc.

THE DESTRUCTION OF DRESDEN by David Irving: From the Introduction by Ira C. Eaker, Lt. Gen. USAF (RET.) and Foreword by Air Marshal Sir Robert Saundby. Copyright © 1963 by William Kimber and Co. Limited. Reprinted by permission of Holt, Rinehart and Winston, Inc. and William Kimber and Co. Limited.

" 'Leven Cent Cotton" by Bob Miller and Emma Dermer: © Copyright 1928, 1929 by MCA Music, a division of MCA Inc. Copyright renewed 1955, 1956 and assigned to MCA Music, a division of MCA Inc. Used by permission.

The cattle are lowing,
The Baby awakes.
But the little Lord Jesus
No crying He makes.

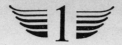

All this happened, more or less. The war parts, anyway, are pretty much true. One guy I knew really *was* shot in Dresden for taking a teapot that wasn't his. Another guy I knew really *did* threaten to have his personal enemies killed by hired gunmen after the war. And so on. I've changed all the names.

I really *did* go back to Dresden with Guggenheim money (God love it) in 1967. It looked a lot like Dayton, Ohio, more open spaces than Dayton has. There must be tons of human bone meal in the ground.

I went back there with an old war buddy, Bernard V. O'Hare, and we made friends with a cab driver, who took us to the slaughterhouse where we had been locked up at night as prisoners of war. His name was Gerhard Müller. He told us that he was a prisoner of the Americans for a while. We asked him how it was to live under Communism, and he said that it was terrible at first, because everybody had to work so hard, and because there wasn't much shelter or food or clothing. But things were much better now. He had a pleasant little apartment, and his daughter was getting an excellent education. His mother was incinerated in the Dresden fire-storm. So it goes.

He sent O'Hare a postcard at Christmastime, and here is what it said:

"I wish you and your family also as to your friend Merry Christmas and a happy New Year and I hope that we'll meet again in a world of peace and freedom in the taxi cab if the accident will."

I like that very much: "If the accident will."

I would hate to tell you what this lousy little book cost me in money and anxiety and time. When I got home from the Second World War twenty-three years ago, I thought it would be easy for me to write about the destruction of Dresden, since all I would have to do would be to report what I had seen. And I thought, too, that it would be a masterpiece or at least make me a lot of money, since the subject was so big.

But not many words about Dresden came from my mind then—not enough of them to make a book, anyway. And not many words come now, either, when I have become an old fart with his memories and his Pall Malls, with his sons full grown.

I think of how useless the Dresden part of my memory has been, and yet how tempting Dresden has been to write about, and I am reminded of the famous limerick:

> There was a young man from Stamboul,
> Who soliloquized thus to his tool:
> "You took all my wealth
> And you ruined my health,
> And now you won't *pee,* you old fool."

And I'm reminded, too, of the song that goes:

> My name is Yon Yonson,
> I work in Wisconsin,
> I work in a lumbermill there.
> The people I meet when I walk down the street,

They say, "What's your name?"
And I say,
"My name is Yon Yonson,
I work in Wisconsin . . ."

And so on to infinity.

Over the years, people I've met have often asked me what I'm working on, and I've usually replied that the main thing was a book about Dresden.

I said that to Harrison Starr, the movie-maker, one time, and he raised his eyebrows and inquired, "Is it an anti-war book?"

"Yes," I said. "I guess."

"You know what I say to people when I hear they're writing anti-war books?"

"No. What *do* you say, Harrison Starr?"

"I say, 'Why don't you write an anti-*glacier* book instead?'"

What he meant, of course, was that there would always be wars, that they were as easy to stop as glaciers. I believe that, too.

And, even if wars didn't keep coming like glaciers, there would still be plain old death.

When I was somewhat younger, working on my famous Dresden book, I asked an old war buddy named Bernard V. O'Hare if I could come to see him. He was a district attorney in Pennsylvania. I was a writer on Cape Cod. We had been privates in the war, infantry scouts. We had never expected to make any money after the war, but we were doing quite well.

I had the Bell Telephone Company find him for me. They are wonderful that way. I have this disease late at night sometimes, involving alcohol and the telephone. I get drunk, and I drive my wife away with a breath like mustard gas and roses. And then, speaking gravely and elegantly into the telephone, I ask the telephone operators to connect me with this friend or that one, from whom I have not heard in years.

I got O'Hare on the line in this way. He is short and I am tall. We were Mutt and Jeff in the war. We were captured together in the war. I told him who I was on the telephone. He had no trouble believing it. He was up. He was reading. Everybody else in his house was asleep.

"Listen—" I said, "I'm writing this book about Dresden. I'd like some help remembering stuff. I wonder if I could come down and see you, and we could drink and talk and remember."

He was unenthusiastic. He said he couldn't remember much. He told me, though, to come ahead.

"I think the climax of the book will be the execution of poor old Edgar Derby," I said. "The irony is *so* great. A whole city gets burned down, and thousands and thousands of people are killed. And then this one American foot soldier is arrested in the ruins for taking a teapot. And he's given a regular trial, and then he's shot by a firing squad."

"Um," said O'Hare.

"Don't you think that's really where the climax should come?"

"I don't know anything about it," he said. "That's your trade, not mine."

As a trafficker in climaxes and thrills and characterization and wonderful dialogue and suspense and confrontations, I had outlined the Dresden story many times. The best outline I ever made, or anyway the prettiest one, was on the back of a roll of wallpaper.

I used my daughter's crayons, a different color for each main character. One end of the wallpaper was the beginning of the story, and the other end was the end, and then there was all that middle part, which was the middle. And the blue line met the red line and then the yellow line, and the yellow line stopped because the character represented by the yellow line was dead. And so on. The destruction of Dresden was represented by a vertical band of orange cross-hatching, and all the lines that were still alive passed through it, came out the other side.

The end, where all the lines stopped, was a beetfield on the Elbe, outside of Halle. The rain was coming down. The war in Europe had been over for a couple of weeks. We were formed in ranks, with Russian soldiers guarding us—Englishmen, Americans, Dutchmen, Belgians, Frenchmen, Canadians, South Africans, New Zealanders, Australians, thousands of us about to stop being prisoners of war.

And on the other side of the field were thousands of Russians and Poles and Yugoslavians and so on guarded by American soldiers. An exchange was made there in the rain—one for one. O'Hare and I climbed into the back of an American truck with a lot of others. O'Hare didn't have any souvenirs. Almost everybody else did. I had a ceremonial Luftwaffe saber, still do. The rabid little American I call Paul Lazzaro in this book had about a quart of diamonds and emeralds and rubies and so on. He had taken these from dead people in the cellars of Dresden. So it goes.

An idiotic Englishman, who had lost all his teeth somewhere, had his souvenir in a canvas bag. The bag was resting on my insteps. He would peek into the bag every

[5]

now and then, and he would roll his eyes and swivel his scrawny neck, trying to catch people looking covetously at his bag. And he would bounce the bag on my insteps.

I thought this bouncing was accidental. But I was mistaken. He *had* to show somebody what was in the bag, and he had decided he could trust me. He caught my eye, winked, opened the bag. There was a plaster model of the Eiffel Tower in there. It was painted gold. It had a clock in it.

"There's a smashin' thing," he said.

And we were flown to a rest camp in France, where we were fed chocolate malted milkshakes and other rich foods until we were all covered with baby fat. Then we were sent home, and I married a pretty girl who was covered with baby fat, too.

And we had babies.

And they're all grown up now, and I'm an old fart with his memories and his Pall Malls. My name is Yon Yonson, I work in Wisconsin, I work in a lumbermill there.

Sometimes I try to call up old girl friends on the telephone late at night, after my wife has gone to bed. "Operator, I wonder if you could give me the number of a Mrs. So-and-So. I think she lives at such-and-such."

"I'm sorry, sir. There is no such listing."

"Thanks, Operator. Thanks just the same."

And I let the dog out, or I let him in, and we talk some. I let him know I like him, and he lets me know he likes me. He doesn't mind the smell of mustard gas and roses.

"You're all right, Sandy," I'll say to the dog. "You know that, Sandy? You're O.K."

Sometimes I'll turn on the radio and listen to a talk

program from Boston or New York. I can't stand recorded music if I've been drinking a good deal.

Sooner or later I go to bed, and my wife asks me what time it is. She always has to know the time. Sometimes I don't know, and I say, "Search *me*."

I think about my education sometimes. I went to the University of Chicago for a while after the Second World War. I was a student in the Department of Anthropology. At that time, they were teaching that there was absolutely no difference between anybody. They may be teaching that still.

Another thing they taught was that nobody was ridiculous or bad or disgusting. Shortly before my father died, he said to me, "You know—you never wrote a story with a villain in it."

I told him that was one of the things I learned in college after the war.

While I was studying to be an anthropologist, I was also working as a police reporter for the famous Chicago City News Bureau for twenty-eight dollars a week. One time they switched me from the night shift to the day shift, so I worked sixteen hours straight. We were supported by all the newspapers in town, and the AP and the UP and all that. And we would cover the courts and the police stations and the Fire Department and the Coast Guard out on Lake Michigan and all that. We were connected to the institutions that supported us by means of pneumatic tubes which ran under the streets of Chicago.

Reporters would telephone in stories to writers wearing headphones, and the writers would stencil the stories on mimeograph sheets. The stories were mimeographed and

[7]

stuffed into the brass and velvet cartridges which the pneumatic tubes ate. The very toughest reporters and writers were women who had taken over the jobs of men who'd gone to war.

And the first story I covered I had to dictate over the telephone to one of those beastly girls. It was about a young veteran who had taken a job running an old-fashioned elevator in an office building. The elevator door on the first floor was ornamental iron lace. Iron ivy snaked in and out of the holes. There was an iron twig with two iron lovebirds perched upon it.

This veteran decided to take his car into the basement, and he closed the door and started down, but his wedding ring was caught in all the ornaments. So he was hoisted into the air and the floor of the car went down, dropped out from under him, and the top of the car squashed him. So it goes.

So I phoned this in, and the woman who was going to cut the stencil asked me, "What did his wife say?"

"She doesn't know yet," I said. "It just happened."

"Call her up and get a statement."

"What?"

"Tell her you're Captain Finn of the Police Department. Say you have some sad news. Give her the news, and see what she says."

So I did. She said about what you would expect her to say. There was a baby. And so on.

When I got back to the office, the woman writer asked me, just for her own information, what the squashed guy had looked like when he was squashed.

I told her.

"Did it bother you?" she said. She was eating a Three Musketeers Candy Bar.

[8]

"Heck no, Nancy," I said. "I've seen lots worse than that in the war."

Even then I was supposedly writing a book about Dresden. It wasn't a famous air raid back then in America. Not many Americans knew how much worse it had been than Hiroshima, for instance. I didn't know that, either. There hadn't been much publicity.

I happened to tell a University of Chicago professor at a cocktail party about the raid as I had seen it, about the book I would write. He was a member of a thing called The Committee on Social Thought. And he told me about the concentration camps, and about how the Germans had made soap and candles out of the fat of dead Jews and so on.

All I could say was, "I know, I know. I *know*."

World War Two had certainly made everybody very tough. And I became a public relations man for General Electric in Schenectady, New York, and a volunteer fireman in the village of Alplaus, where I bought my first home. My boss there was one of the toughest guys I ever hope to meet. He had been a lieutenant colonel in public relations in Baltimore. While I was in Schenectady he joined the Dutch Reformed Church, which is a very tough church, indeed.

He used to ask me sneeringly sometimes why I hadn't been an officer, as though I'd done something wrong.

My wife and I had lost our baby fat. Those were our scrawny years. We had a lot of scrawny veterans and their scrawny wives for friends. The nicest veterans in Schenectady, I thought, the kindest and funniest ones, the ones who hated war the most, were the ones who'd really fought.

I wrote the Air Force back then, asking for details about the raid on Dresden, who ordered it, how many planes did it, why they did it, what desirable results there had been and so on. I was answered by a man who, like myself, was in public relations. He said that he was sorry, but that the information was top secret still.

I read the letter out loud to my wife, and I said, "Secret? My God—from *whom?*"

We were United World Federalists back then. I don't know what we are now. Telephoners, I guess. We telephone a lot—or *I* do, anyway, late at night.

A couple of weeks after I telephoned my old war buddy, Bernard V. O'Hare, I really *did* go to see him. That must have been in 1964 or so—whatever the last year was for the New York World's Fair. *Eheu, fugaces labuntur anni.* My name is Yon Yonson. There was a young man from Stamboul.

I took two little girls with me, my daughter, Nanny, and her best friend, Allison Mitchell. They had never been off Cape Cod before. When we saw a river, we had to stop so they could stand by it and think about it for a while. They had never seen water in that long and narrow, unsalted form before. The river was the Hudson. There were carp in there and we saw them. They were as big as atomic submarines.

We saw waterfalls, too, streams jumping off cliffs into the valley of the Delaware. There were lots of things to stop and see—and then it was time to go, always time to go. The little girls were wearing white party dresses and black party shoes, so strangers would know at once how nice they were. "Time to go, girls," I'd say. And we would go.

And the sun went down, and we had supper in an Italian place, and then I knocked on the front door of the beautiful stone house of Bernard V. O'Hare. I was carrying a bottle of Irish whiskey like a dinner bell.

I met his nice wife, Mary, to whom I dedicate this book. I dedicate it to Gerhard Müller, the Dresden taxi driver, too. Mary O'Hare is a trained nurse, which is a lovely thing for a woman to be.

Mary admired the two little girls I'd brought, mixed them in with her own children, sent them all upstairs to play games and watch television. It was only after the children were gone that I sensed that Mary didn't like me or didn't like *something* about the night. She was polite but chilly.

"It's a nice cozy house you have here," I said, and it really was.

"I've fixed up a place where you can talk and not be bothered," she said.

"Good," I said, and I imagined two leather chairs near a fire in a paneled room, where two old soldiers could drink and talk. But she took us into the kitchen. She had put two straight-backed chairs at a kitchen table with a white porcelain top. That table top was screaming with reflected light from a two-hundred-watt bulb overhead. Mary had prepared an operating room. She put only one glass on it, which was for me. She explained that O'Hare couldn't drink the hard stuff since the war.

So we sat down. O'Hare was embarrassed, but he wouldn't tell me what was wrong. I couldn't imagine what it was about me that could burn up Mary so. I was a family man. I'd been married only once. I wasn't a drunk. I hadn't done her husband any dirt in the war.

She fixed herself a Coca-Cola, made a lot of noise banging the ice-cube tray in the stainless steel sink. Then she went into another part of the house. But she wouldn't sit still. She was moving all over the house, opening and shutting doors, even moving furniture around to work off anger.

I asked O'Hare what I'd said or done to make her act that way.

"It's all right," he said. "Don't worry about it. It doesn't have anything to do with you." That was kind of him. He was lying. It had everything to do with me.

So we tried to ignore Mary and remember the war. I took a couple of belts of the booze I'd brought. We would chuckle or grin sometimes, as though war stories were coming back, but neither one of us could remember anything good. O'Hare remembered one guy who got into a lot of wine in Dresden, before it was bombed, and we had to take him home in a wheelbarrow. It wasn't much to write a book about. I remembered two Russian soldiers who had looted a clock factory. They had a horse-drawn wagon full of clocks. They were happy and drunk. They were smoking huge cigarettes they had rolled in newspaper.

That was about *it* for memories, and Mary was still making noise. She finally came out in the kitchen again for another Coke. She took another tray of ice cubes from the refrigerator, banged it in the sink, even though there was already plenty of ice out.

Then she turned to me, let me see how angry she was, and that the anger was for me. She had been talking to herself, so what she said was a fragment of a much larger conversation. "You were just *babies* then!" she said.

"What?" I said.

"You were just babies in the war—like the ones up-stairs!"

I nodded that this was true. We *had* been foolish virgins in the war, right at the end of childhood.

"But you're not going to write it that way, are you." This wasn't a question. It was an accusation.

"I—I don't know," I said.

"Well, *I* know," she said. "You'll pretend you were men instead of babies, and you'll be played in the movies by Frank Sinatra and John Wayne or some of those other glamorous, war-loving, dirty old men. And war will look just wonderful, so we'll have a lot more of them. And they'll be fought by babies like the babies upstairs."

So then I understood. It was war that made her so angry. She didn't want her babies or anybody else's babies killed in wars. And she thought wars were partly encouraged by books and movies.

So I held up my right hand and I made her a promise: "Mary," I said, "I don't think this book of mine is ever going to be finished. I must have written five thousand pages by now, and thrown them all away. If I ever do finish it, though, I give you my word of honor: there won't be a part for Frank Sinatra or John Wayne.

"I tell you what," I said, "I'll call it 'The Children's Crusade.'"

She was my friend after that.

O'Hare and I gave up on remembering, went into the living room, talked about other things. We became curious about the real Children's Crusade, so O'Hare looked it up in a book he had, *Extraordinary Popular Delusions and the Madness of Crowds,* by Charles Mackay, LL. D. It was first published in London in 1841.

Mackay had a low opinion of *all* Crusades. The Children's Crusade struck him as only slightly more sordid than the ten Crusades for grown-ups. O'Hare read this handsome passage out loud:

History in her solemn page informs us that the crusaders were but ignorant and savage men, that their motives were those of bigotry unmitigated, and that their pathway was one of blood and tears. Romance, on the other hand, dilates upon their piety and heroism, and portrays, in her most glowing and impassioned hues, their virtue and magnanimity, the imperishable honor they acquired for themselves, and the great services they rendered to Christianity.

And then O'Hare read this: *Now what was the grand result of all these struggles? Europe expended millions of her treasures, and the blood of two million of her people; and a handful of quarrelsome knights retained possession of Palestine for about one hundred years!*

Mackay told us that the Children's Crusade started in 1213, when two monks got the idea of raising armies of children in Germany and France, and selling them in North Africa as slaves. Thirty thousand children volunteered, thinking they were going to Palestine. *They were no doubt idle and deserted children who generally swarm in great cities, nurtured on vice and daring,* said Mackay, *and ready for anything.*

Pope Innocent the Third thought they were going to Palestine, too, and he was thrilled. "These children are awake while we are asleep!" he said.

Most of the children were shipped out of Marseilles, and about half of them drowned in shipwrecks. The other half got to North Africa where they were sold.

Through a misunderstanding, some children reported for duty at Genoa, where no slave ships were waiting. They were fed and sheltered and questioned kindly by good people there—then given a little money and a lot of advice and sent back home.

"Hooray for the good people of Genoa," said Mary O'Hare.

I slept that night in one of the children's bedrooms. O'Hare had put a book for me on the bedside table. It was *Dresden, History, Stage and Gallery,* by Mary Endell. It was published in 1908, and its introduction began:

It is hoped that this little book will make itself useful. It attempts to give to an English-reading public a bird's-eye view of how Dresden came to look as it does, architecturally; of how it expanded musically, through the genius of a few men, to its present bloom; and it calls attention to certain permanent landmarks in art that make its Gallery the resort of those seeking lasting impressions.

I read some history further on:

Now, in 1760, Dresden underwent siege by the Prussians. On the fifteenth of July began the cannonade. The Picture-Gallery took fire. Many of the paintings had been transported to the Königstein, but some were seriously injured by splinters of bombshells,—notably Francia's "Baptism of Christ." Furthermore, the stately Kreuzkirche tower, from which the enemy's movements had been watched day and night, stood in flames. It later succumbed. In sturdy contrast with the pitiful fate of the Kreuzkirche, stood the Frauenkirche, from the curves of whose stone dome the Prussian bombs rebounded like rain. Friederich was obliged finally to give up the siege, because he learned of the fall of Glatz, the critical point of his new conquests.

[15]

"We must be off to Silesia, so that we do not lose every-thing."

The devastation of Dresden was boundless. When Goethe as a young student visited the city, he still found sad ruins: "Von der Kuppel der Frauenkirche sah ich diese leidigen Trümmer zwischen die schöne städtische Ord-nung hineingesät; da rühmte mir der Küster die Kunst des Baumeisters, welcher Kirche und Kuppel auf einen so unerwünschten Fall schon eingerichtet und bombenfest erbaut hatte. Der gute Sakristan deutete mir alsdann auf Ruinene nach allen Seiten und sagte bedenklich lakonisch: Das hat der Feind gethan!"

The two little girls and I crossed the Delaware River where George Washington had crossed it, the next morn-ing. We went to the New York World's Fair, saw what the past had been like, according to the Ford Motor Car Company and Walt Disney, saw what the future would be like, according to General Motors.

And I asked myself about the present: how wide it was, how deep it was, how much was mine to keep.

I taught creative writing in the famous Writers Work-shop at the University of Iowa for a couple of years after that. I got into some perfectly beautiful trouble, got out of it again. I taught in the afternoons. In the mornings I wrote. I was not to be disturbed. I was working on my famous book about Dresden.

And somewhere in there a nice man named Seymour Lawrence gave me a three-book contract, and I said, "O.K., the first of the three will be my famous book about Dresden."

The friends of Seymour Lawrence call him "Sam." And I say to Sam now: "Sam—here's the book."

It is so short and jumbled and jangled, Sam, because there is nothing intelligent to say about a massacre. Everybody is supposed to be dead, to never say anything or want anything ever again. Everything is supposed to be very quiet after a massacre, and it always is, except for the birds.

And what do the birds say? All there is to say about a massacre, things like *"Poo-tee-weet?"*

I have told my sons that they are not under any circumstances to take part in massacres, and that the news of massacres of enemies is not to fill them with satisfaction or glee.

I have also told them not to work for companies which make massacre machinery, and to express contempt for people who think we need machinery like that.

As I've said: I recently went back to Dresden with my friend O'Hare. We had a million laughs in Hamburg and West Berlin and East Berlin and Vienna and Salzburg and Helsinki, and in Leningrad, too. It was very good for me, because I saw a lot of authentic backgrounds for made-up stories which I will write later on. One of them will be "Russian Baroque" and another will be "No Kissing" and another will be "Dollar Bar" and another will be "If the Accident Will," and so on.

And so on.

There was a Lufthansa plane that was supposed to fly from Philadelphia to Boston to Frankfurt. O'Hare was

[17]

supposed to get on in Philadelphia and I was supposed to get on in Boston, and off we'd go. But Boston was socked in, so the plane flew straight to Frankfurt from Philadelphia. And I became a non-person in the Boston fog, and Lufthansa put me in a limousine with some other non-persons and sent us to a motel for a non-night.

The time would not pass. Somebody was playing with the clocks, and not only with the electric clocks, but the wind-up kind, too. The second hand on my watch would twitch once, and a year would pass, and then it would twitch again.

There was nothing I could do about it. As an Earthling, I had to believe whatever clocks said—and calendars.

I had two books with me, which I'd meant to read on the plane. One was *Words for the Wind*, by Theodore Roethke, and this is what I found in there:

> *I wake to sleep, and take my waking slow.*
> *I feel my fate in what I cannot fear.*
> *I learn by going where I have to go.*

My other book was Erika Ostrovsky's *Céline and His Vision*. Céline was a brave French soldier in the First World War—until his skull was cracked. After that he couldn't sleep, and there were noises in his head. He became a doctor, and he treated poor people in the daytime, and he wrote grotesque novels all night. No art is possible without a dance with death, he wrote.

The truth is death, he wrote. *I've fought nicely against it as long as I could . . . danced with it, festooned it, waltzed it around . . . decorated it with streamers, titillated it . . .*

Time obsessed him. Miss Ostrovsky reminded me of the

amazing scene in *Death on the Installment Plan* where Céline wants to stop the bustling of a street crowd. He screams on paper, *Make them stop . . . don't let them move anymore at all . . . There, make them freeze . . . once and for all! . . . So that they won't disappear anymore!*

I looked through the Gideon Bible in my motel room for tales of great destruction. *The sun was risen upon the Earth when Lot entered into Zo-ar,* I read. *Then the Lord rained upon Sodom and upon Gomorrah brimstone and fire from the Lord out of Heaven; and He overthrew those cities, and all the plain, and all the inhabitants of the cities, and that which grew upon the ground.*

So it goes.

Those were vile people in both those cities, as is well known. The world was better off without them.

And Lot's wife, of course, was told not to look back where all those people and their homes had been. But she *did* look back, and I love her for that, because it was so human.

So she was turned to a pillar of salt. So it goes.

People aren't supposed to look back. I'm certainly not going to do it anymore.

I've finished my war book now. The next one I write is going to be fun.

This one is a failure, and had to be, since it was written by a pillar of salt. It begins like this:

Listen:

Billy Pilgrim has come unstuck in time.

It ends like this:

Poo-tee-weet?

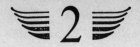

2

Listen:

Billy Pilgrim has come unstuck in time.

Billy has gone to sleep a senile widower and awakened on his wedding day. He has walked through a door in 1955 and come out another one in 1941. He has gone back through that door to find himself in 1963. He has seen his birth and death many times, he says, and pays random visits to all the events in between.

He says.

Billy is spastic in time, has no control over where he is going next, and the trips aren't necessarily fun. He is in a constant state of stage fright, he says, because he never knows what part of his life he is going to have to act in next.

Billy was born in 1922 in Ilium, New York, the only child of a barber there. He was a funny-looking child who became a funny-looking youth—tall and weak, and shaped like a bottle of Coca-Cola. He graduated from Ilium High School in the upper third of his class, and attended night sessions at the Ilium School of Optometry for one semester before being drafted for military service in the Second World War. His father died in a hunting accident during the war. So it goes.

Billy saw service with the infantry in Europe, and was taken prisoner by the Germans. After his honorable discharge from the Army in 1945, Billy again enrolled in the Ilium School of Optometry. During his senior year there, he became engaged to the daughter of the founder and owner of the school, and then suffered a mild nervous collapse.

He was treated in a veteran's hospital near Lake Placid, and was given shock treatments and released. He married his fiancée, finished his education, and was set up in business in Ilium by his father-in-law. Ilium is a particularly good city for optometrists because the General Forge and Foundry Company is there. Every employee is required to own a pair of safety glasses, and to wear them in areas where manufacturing is going on. GF&F has sixty-eight thousand employees in Ilium. That calls for a lot of lenses and a lot of frames.

Frames are where the money is.

Billy became rich. He had two children, Barbara and Robert. In time, his daughter Barbara married another optometrist, and Billy set him up in business. Billy's son Robert had a lot of trouble in high school, but then he joined the famous Green Berets. He straightened out, became a fine young man, and he fought in Vietnam.

Early in 1968, a group of optometrists, with Billy among them, chartered an airplane to fly them from Ilium to an international convention of optometrists in Montreal. The plane crashed on top of Sugarbush Mountain, in Vermont. Everybody was killed but Billy. So it goes.

While Billy was recuperating in a hospital in Vermont,

his wife died accidentally of carbon-monoxide poisoning. So it goes.

When Billy finally got home to Ilium after the airplane crash, he was quiet for a while. He had a terrible scar across the top of his skull. He didn't resume practice. He had a housekeeper. His daughter came over almost every day.

And then, without any warning, Billy went to New York City, and got on an all-night radio program devoted to talk. He told about having come unstuck in time. He said, too, that he had been kidnapped by a flying saucer in 1967. The saucer was from the planet Tralfamadore, he said. He was taken to Tralfamadore, where he was displayed naked in a zoo, he said. He was mated there with a former Earthling movie star named Montana Wildhack.

Some night owls in Ilium heard Billy on the radio, and one of them called Billy's daughter Barbara. Barbara was upset. She and her husband went down to New York and brought Billy home. Billy insisted mildly that everything he had said on the radio was true. He said he had been kidnapped by the Tralfamadorians on the night of his daughter's wedding. He hadn't been missed, he said, because the Tralfamadorians had taken him through a time warp, so that he could be on Tralfamadore for years, and still be away from Earth for only a microsecond.

Another month went by without incident, and then Billy wrote a letter to the Ilium *News Leader,* which the paper published. It described the creatures from Tralfamadore.

The letter said that they were two feet high, and green, and shaped like plumber's friends. Their suction cups were on the ground, and their shafts, which were extremely flexible, usually pointed to the sky. At the top of each shaft was a little hand with a green eye in its palm. The creatures were friendly, and they could see in four dimensions. They pitied Earthlings for being able to see only three. They had many wonderful things to teach Earthlings, especially about time. Billy promised to tell what some of those wonderful things were in his next letter.

Billy was working on his second letter when the first letter was published. The second letter started out like this:

"The most important thing I learned on Tralfamadore was that when a person dies he only *appears* to die. He is still very much alive in the past, so it is very silly for people to cry at his funeral. All moments, past, present, and future, always have existed, always will exist. The Tralfamadorians can look at all the different moments just the way we can look at a stretch of the Rocky Mountains, for instance. They can see how permanent all the moments are, and they can look at any moment that interests them. It is just an illusion we have here on Earth that one moment follows another one, like beads on a string, and that once a moment is gone it is gone forever.

"When a Tralfamadorian sees a corpse, all he thinks is that the dead person is in bad condition in that particular moment, but that the same person is just fine in plenty of other moments. Now, when I myself hear that somebody is dead, I simply shrug and say what the Tralfamadorians say about dead people, which is 'So it goes.' "

And so on.

Billy was working on this letter in the basement rumpus room of his empty house. It was his housekeeper's day off.

There was an old typewriter in the rumpus room. It was a beast. It weighed as much as a storage battery. Billy couldn't carry it very far very easily, which was why he was writing in the rumpus room instead of somewhere else.

The oil burner had quit. A mouse had eaten through the insulation of a wire leading to the thermostat. The temperature in the house was down to fifty degrees, but Billy hadn't noticed. He wasn't warmly dressed, either. He was barefoot, and still in his pajamas and a bathrobe, though it was late afternoon. His bare feet were blue and ivory.

The cockles of Billy's heart, at any rate, were glowing coals. What made them so hot was Billy's belief that he was going to comfort so many people with the truth about time. His door chimes upstairs had been ringing and ringing. It was his daughter Barbara up there, wanting in. Now she let herself in with a key, crossed the floor over his head, calling, "Father? Daddy, where are you?" And so on.

Billy didn't answer her, so she was nearly hysterical, expecting to find his corpse. And then she looked into the very last place there *was* to look—which was the rumpus room.

"Why didn't you answer me when I called?" Barbara wanted to know, standing there in the door of the rumpus room. She had the afternoon paper with her, the one in which Billy described his friends from Tralfamadore.

"I didn't *hear* you," said Billy.

The orchestration of the moment was this: Barbara was only twenty-one years old, but she thought her father was senile, even though he was only forty-six—senile because of damage to his brain in the airplane crash. She also thought that she was head of the family, since she had had to

[24]

manage her mother's funeral, since she had to get a house-keeper for Billy, and all that. Also, Barbara and her husband were having to look after Billy's business interests, which were considerable, since Billy didn't seem to give a damn for business any more. All this responsibility at such an early age made her a bitchy flibbertigibbet. And Billy, meanwhile, was trying to hang onto his dignity, to persuade Barbara and everybody else that he was far from senile, that, on the contrary, he was devoting himself to a calling much higher than mere business.

He was doing nothing less now, he thought, then prescribing corrective lenses for Earthling souls. So many of those souls were lost and wretched, Billy believed, because they could not see as well as his little green friends on Tralfamadore.

"Don't lie to me, Father," said Barbara. "I know perfectly well you heard me when I called." This was a fairly pretty girl, except that she had legs like an Edwardian grand piano. Now she raised hell with him about the letter in the paper. She said he was making a laughing stock of himself and everybody associated with him.

"Father, Father, Father—" said Barbara, "what are we going to *do* with you? Are you going to force us to put you where your mother is?" Billy's mother was still alive. She was in bed in an old people's home called Pine Knoll on the edge of Ilium.

"What is it about my letter that makes you so mad?" Billy wanted to know.

"It's all just crazy. None of it's true!"

"It's all true." Billy's anger was not going to rise with hers. He never got mad at anything. He was wonderful that way.

[25]

"There is no such planet as Tralfamadore."

"It can't be detected from Earth, if that's what you mean," said Billy. "Earth can't be detected from Tralfamadore, as far as that goes. They're both very small. They're very far apart."

"Where did you get a crazy name like 'Tralfamadore?'"

"That's what the creatures who live there *call* it."

"Oh God," said Barbara, and she turned her back on him. She celebrated frustration by clapping her hands. "May I ask you a simple question?"

"Of course."

"Why is it you never mentioned any of this before the airplane crash?"

"I didn't think the time was *ripe*."

And so on. Billy says that he first came unstuck in time in 1944, long before his trip to Tralfamadore. The Tralfamadorians didn't have anything to do with his coming unstuck. They were simply able to give him insights into what was really going on.

Billy first came unstuck while World War Two was in progress. Billy was a chaplain's assistant in the war. A chaplain's assistant is customarily a figure of fun in the American Army. Billy was no exception. He was powerless to harm the enemy or to help his friends. In fact, he had no friends. He was a valet to a preacher, expected no promotions or medals, bore no arms, and had a meek faith in a loving Jesus which most soldiers found putrid.

While on maneuvers in South Carolina, Billy played hymns he knew from childhood, played them on a little black organ which was waterproof. It had thirty-nine keys and two stops—*vox humana* and *vox celeste*. Billy also had charge of a portable altar, an olive-drab attaché case with telescoping legs. It was lined with crimson plush, and nestled in that passionate plush were an anodized aluminum cross and a Bible.

The altar and the organ were made by a vacuum-cleaner company in Camden, New Jersey—and said so.

One time on maneuvers Billy was playing "A Mighty Fortress Is Our God," with music by Johann Sebastian Bach and words by Martin Luther. It was Sunday morning. Billy and his chaplain had gathered a congregation of about fifty soldiers on a Carolina hillside. An umpire appeared. There were umpires everywhere, men who said who was winning or losing the theoretical battle, who was alive and who was dead.

The umpire had comical news. The congregation had been theoretically spotted from the air by a theoretical enemy. They were all theoretically dead now. The theoretical corpses laughed and ate a hearty noontime meal.

Remembering this incident years later, Billy was struck by what a Tralfamadorian adventure with death that had been, to be dead and to eat at the same time.

Toward the end of maneuvers, Billy was given an emergency furlough home because his father, a barber in Ilium, New York, was shot dead by a friend while they were out hunting deer. So it goes.

When Billy got back from his furlough, there were orders for him to go overseas. He was needed in the headquarters company of an infantry regiment fighting in Luxembourg. The regimental chaplain's assistant had been killed in action. So it goes.

[27]

When Billy joined the regiment, it was in the process of being destroyed by the Germans in the famous Battle of the Bulge. Billy never even got to meet the chaplain he was supposed to assist, was never even issued a steel helmet and combat boots. This was in December of 1944, during the last mighty German attack of the war.

Billy survived, but he was a dazed wanderer far behind the new German lines. Three other wanderers, not quite so dazed, allowed Billy to tag along. Two of them were scouts, and one was an antitank gunner. They were without food or maps. Avoiding Germans, they were delivering themselves into rural silences ever more profound. They ate snow.

They went Indian file. First came the scouts, clever, graceful, quiet. They had rifles. Next came the antitank gunner, clumsy and dense, warning Germans away with a Colt .45 automatic in one hand and a trench knife in the other.

Last came Billy Pilgrim, empty-handed, bleakly ready for death. Billy was preposterous—six feet and three inches tall, with a chest and shoulders like a box of kitchen matches. He had no helmet, no overcoat, no weapon, and no boots. On his feet were cheap, low-cut civilian shoes which he had bought for his father's funeral. Billy had lost a heel, which made him bob up-and-down, up-and-down. The involuntary dancing, up and down, up and down, made his hip joints sore.

Billy was wearing a thin field jacket, a shirt and trousers of scratchy wool, and long underwear that was soaked with sweat. He was the only one of the four who had a beard. It was a random, bristly beard, and some of the bristles were white, even though Billy was only twenty-one years old.

He was also going bald. Wind and cold and violent exercise had turned his face crimson.

He didn't look like a soldier at all. He looked like a filthy flamingo.

And on the third day of wandering, somebody shot at the four from far away—shot four times as they crossed a narrow brick road. One shot was for the scouts. The next one was for the antitank gunner, whose name was Roland Weary.

The third bullet was for the filthy flamingo, who stopped dead center in the road when the lethal bee buzzed past his ear. Billy stood there politely, giving the marksman another chance. It was his addled understanding of the rules of warfare that the marksman *should* be given a second chance. The next shot missed Billy's kneecaps by inches, going end-on-end, from the sound of it.

Roland Weary and the scouts were safe in a ditch, and Weary growled at Billy, "Get out of the road, you dumb motherfucker." The last word was still a novelty in the speech of white people in 1944. It was fresh and astonishing to Billy, who had never fucked anybody—and it did its job. It woke him up and got him off the road.

"Saved your life again, you dumb bastard," Weary said to Billy in the ditch. He had been saving Billy's life for days, cursing him, kicking him, slapping him, making him move. It was absolutely necessary that cruelty be used, because Billy wouldn't do anything to save himself. Billy wanted to quit. He was cold, hungry, embarrassed, incompetent. He could scarcely distinguish between sleep and wakefulness now, on the third day, found no important differences, either, between walking and standing still.

He wished everybody would leave him alone. "You guys go on without me," he said again and again.

Weary was as new to war as Billy. He was a replacement, too. As a part of a gun crew, he had helped to fire one shot in anger—from a 57-millimeter antitank gun. The gun made a ripping sound like the opening of the zipper on the fly of God Almighty. The gun lapped up snow and vegetation with a blowtorch thirty feet long. The flame left a black arrow on the ground, showing the Germans exactly where the gun was hidden. The shot was a miss.

What had been missed was a Tiger tank. It swiveled its 88-millimeter snout around sniffingly, saw the arrow on the ground. It fired. It killed everybody on the gun crew but Weary. So it goes.

Roland Weary was only eighteen, was at the end of an unhappy childhood spent mostly in Pittsburgh, Pennsylvania. He had been unpopular in Pittsburgh. He had been unpopular because he was stupid and fat and mean, and smelled like bacon no matter how much he washed. He was always being ditched in Pittsburgh by people who did not want him with them.

It made Weary sick to be ditched. When Weary was ditched, he would find somebody who was even more unpopular than himself, and he would horse around with that person for a while, pretending to be friendly. And then he would find some pretext for beating the shit out of him.

It was a pattern. It was a crazy, sexy, murderous relationship Weary entered into with people he eventually beat up. He told them about his father's collection of guns and swords and torture instruments and leg irons and so on. Weary's father, who was a plumber, actually did collect such things, and his collection was insured for four thousand dollars. He wasn't alone. He belonged to a big club composed of people who collected things like that.

Weary's father once gave Weary's mother a Spanish thumbscrew in working condition—for a kitchen paperweight. Another time he gave her a table lamp whose base was a model one foot high of the famous "Iron Maiden of Nuremburg." The real Iron Maiden was a medieval torture instrument, a sort of boiler which was shaped like a woman on the outside—and lined with spikes. The front of the woman was composed of two hinged doors. The idea was to put a criminal inside and then close the doors slowly. There were two special spikes where his eyes would be. There was a drain in the bottom to let out all the blood.

So it goes.

Weary had told Billy Pilgrim about the Iron Maiden, about the drain in her bottom—and what that was for. He had talked to Billy about dum-dums. He told him about his father's Derringer pistol, which could be carried in a vest pocket, which was yet capable of making a hole in a man "which a bull bat could fly through without touching either wing."

Weary scornfully bet Billy one time that he didn't even know what a blood gutter was. Billy guessed that it was the drain in the bottom of the Iron Maiden, but that was wrong. A blood gutter, Billy learned, was the shallow groove in the side of the blade of a sword or bayonet.

Weary told Billy about neat tortures he'd read about or seen in the movies or heard on the radio—about other neat tortures he himself had invented. One of the inventions was sticking a dentist's drill into a guy's ear. He asked Billy what he thought the worst form of execution was. Billy had no opinion. The correct answer turned out to be this: "You stake a guy out on an anthill in the desert—see? He's facing upward, and you put honey all over his balls and pecker, and you cut off his eyelids so he has to stare at the sun till he dies." So it goes.

Now, lying in the ditch with Billy and the scouts after having been shot at, Weary made Billy take a very close look at his trench knife. It wasn't government issue. It was a present from his father. It had a ten-inch blade that was triangular in cross section. Its grip consisted of brass knuckles, was a chain of rings through which Weary slipped his stubby fingers. The rings weren't simple. They bristled with spikes.

Weary laid the spikes along Billy's cheek, roweled the cheek with savagely affectionate restraint. "How'd you like to be hit with this—hm? Hmmmmmmmmmm?" he wanted to know.

"I wouldn't," said Billy.

"Know why the blade's triangular?"

"No."

"Makes a wound that won't close up."

"Oh."

"Makes a three-sided hole in a guy. You stick an ordinary knife in a guy—makes a slit. Right? A slit closes right up. Right?"

"Right."

"Shit. What do you know? What the hell they teach in college?"

"I wasn't there very long," said Billy, which was true. He had had only six months of college, and the college hadn't been a regular college, either. It had been the night school of the Ilium School of Optometry.

"Joe College," said Weary scathingly.

Billy shrugged.

"There's more to life than what you read in books," said Weary. "You'll find that out."

Billy made no reply to this, either, there in the ditch, since he didn't want the conversation to go on any longer than necessary. He was dimly tempted to say, though, that he knew a thing or two about gore. Billy, after all, had contemplated torture and hideous wounds at the beginning and the end of nearly every day of his childhood. Billy had an extremely gruesome crucifix hanging on the wall of his little bedroom in Ilium. A military surgeon would have admired the clinical fidelity of the artist's rendition of all Christ's wounds—the spear wound, the thorn wounds, the holes that were made by the iron spikes. Billy's Christ died horribly. He was pitiful.

So it goes.

Billy wasn't a Catholic, even though he grew up with a ghastly crucifix on the wall. His father had no religion. His mother was a substitute organist for several churches around town. She took Billy with her whenever she played, taught him to play a little, too. She said she was going to join a church as soon as she decided which one was right.

She never *did* decide. She did develop a terrific hankering for a crucifix, though. And she bought one from a Santa Fe gift shop during a trip the little family made out West during the Great Depression. Like so many Americans, she was trying to construct a life that made sense from things she found in gift shops.

And the crucifix went up on the wall of Billy Pilgrim.

The two scouts, loving the walnut stocks of their rifles in the ditch, whispered that it was time to move out again. Ten minutes had gone by without anybody's coming to see if they were hit or not, to finish them off. Whoever had shot was evidently far away and all alone.

And the four crawled out of the ditch without drawing any more fire. They crawled into a forest like the big, unlucky mammals they were. Then they stood up and began to walk quickly. The forest was dark and old. The pines were planted in ranks and files. There was no undergrowth. Four inches of unmarked snow blanketed the ground. The Americans had no choice but to leave trails in the snow as unambiguous as diagrams in a book on ballroom dancing—*step, slide, rest—step, slide, rest.*

"Close it up and keep it closed!" Roland Weary warned Billy Pilgrim as they moved out. Weary looked like Tweedledum or Tweedledee, all bundled up for battle. He was short and thick.

He had every piece of equipment he had ever been issued, every present he'd received from home: helmet, helmet liner, wool cap, scarf, gloves, cotton undershirt, woolen undershirt, wool shirt, sweater, blouse, jacket, overcoat, cotton underpants, woolen underpants, woolen trousers, cotton socks, woolen socks, combat boots, gas mask, canteen, mess kit, first-aid kit, trench knife, blanket, shelter-half, raincoat, bullet-proof Bible, a pamphlet entitled "Know Your Enemy," another pamphlet entitled "Why We Fight," and another pamphlet of German phrases rendered in English phonetics, which would enable Weary to ask Germans questions such as "Where is your headquarters?" and "How many howitzers have you?" or to tell them, "Surrender. Your situation is hopeless," and so on.

Weary had a block of balsa wood which was supposed to be a foxhole pillow. He had a prophylactic kit containing two tough condoms "For the Prevention of Disease Only!"

He had a whistle he wasn't going to show anybody until he got promoted to corporal. He had a dirty picture of a woman attempting sexual intercourse with a Shetland pony. He had made Billy Pilgrim admire that picture several times.

The woman and the pony were posed before velvet draperies which were fringed with deedlee-balls. They were flanked by Doric columns. In front of one column was a potted palm. The picture that Weary had was a print of the first dirty photograph in history. The word *photography* was first used in 1839, and it was in that year, too, that Louis J. M. Daguerre revealed to the French Academy that an image formed on a silvered metal plate covered with a thin film of silver iodide could be developed in the presence of mercury vapor.

In 1841, only two years later, an assistant to Daguerre, André Le Fèvre, was arrested in the Tuileries Gardens for attempting to sell a gentleman a picture of the woman and the pony. That was where Weary bought his picture, too—in the Tuileries. Le Fèvre argued that the picture was fine art, and that his intention was to make Greek mythology come alive. He said the columns and the potted palm proved that.

When asked which myth he meant to represent, Le Fèvre replied that there were thousands of myths like that, with the woman a mortal and the pony a god.

He was sentenced to six months in prison. He died there of pneumonia. So it goes.

Billy and the scouts were skinny people. Roland Weary had fat to burn. He was a roaring furnace under all his layers of wool and straps and canvas. He had so much energy that he bustled back and forth between Billy and the scouts, delivering dumb messages which nobody had sent and which nobody was pleased to receive. He also began to suspect, since he was so much busier than anybody else, that he was the leader.

He was so hot and bundled up, in fact, that he had no sense of danger. His vision of the outside world was limited to what he could see through a narrow slit between the rim of his helmet and his scarf from home, which concealed his baby face from the bridge of his nose on down. He was so snug in there that he was able to pretend that he was safe at home, having survived the war, and that he was telling his parents and his sister a true war story—whereas the true war story was still going on.

Weary's version of the true war story went like this: There was a big German attack, and Weary and his anti-tank buddies fought like hell until everybody was killed but Weary. So it goes. And then Weary tied in with two scouts, and they became close friends immediately, and they decided to fight their way back to their own lines. They were going to travel fast. They were damned if they'd surrender. They shook hands all around. They called themselves "The Three Musketeers."

But then this damn college kid, who was so weak he shouldn't even have been in the army, asked if he could come along. He didn't even have a gun or a knife. He didn't even have a helmet or a cap. He couldn't even walk right—kept bobbing up-and-down, up-and-down, driving everybody crazy, giving their position away. He was pitiful. The Three Musketeers pushed and carried and dragged the college kid all the way back to their own lines, Weary's story went. They saved his God-damned hide for him.

In real life, Weary was retracing his steps, trying to find out what had happened to Billy. He had told the scouts to wait while he went back for the college bastard. He passed under a low branch now. It hit the top of his helmet with a *clonk*. Weary didn't hear it. Somewhere a big dog was barking. Weary didn't hear that, either. His war story was at a very exciting point. An officer was congratulating the Three Musketeers, telling them that he was going to put them in for Bronze Stars.

"Anything else I can do for you boys?" said the officer.

"Yes, sir," said one of the scouts. "We'd like to stick together for the rest of the war, sir. Is there some way you can fix it so nobody will ever break up the Three Musketeers?"

Billy Pilgrim had stopped in the forest. He was leaning against a tree with his eyes closed. His head was tilted back and his nostrils were flaring. He was like a poet in the Parthenon.

This was when Billy first came unstuck in time. His attention began to swing grandly through the full arc of his life, passing into death, which was violet light. There wasn't anybody else there, or any thing. There was just violet light—and a hum.

An then Billy swung into life again, going backwards until he was in pre-birth, which was red light and bubbling sounds. And then he swung into life again and stopped. He was a little boy taking a shower with his hairy father at the Ilium Y.M.C.A. He smelled chlorine from the swimming pool next door, heard the springboard boom.

Little Billy was terrified, because his father had said Billy was going to learn to swim by the method of sink-or-swim. His father was going to throw Billy into the deep end, and Billy was going to damn well swim.

It was like an execution. Billy was numb as his father carried him from the shower room to the pool. His eyes were closed. When he opened his eyes, he was on the bottom of the pool, and there was beautiful music everywhere. He lost consciousness, but the music went on. He dimly sensed that somebody was rescuing him. Billy resented that.

From there he traveled in time to 1965. He was forty-one years old, and he was visiting his decrepit mother at Pine Knoll, an old people's home he had put her in only a month before. She had caught pneumonia, and wasn't expected to live. She did live, though, for years after that.

Her voice was nearly gone, so, in order to hear her, Billy had to put his ear right next to her papery lips. She evidently had something very important to say.

"How . . . ?" she began, and she stopped. She was too tired. She hoped that she wouldn't have to say the rest of the sentence, that Billy would finish it for her.

But Billy had no idea what was on her mind. "How *what,* Mother?" he prompted.

She swallowed hard, shed some tears. Then she gathered energy from all over her ruined body, even from her toes and fingertips. At last she had accumulated enough to whisper this complete sentence:

"How did I get so *old?*"

Billy's antique mother passed out, and Billy was led from the room by a pretty nurse. The body of an old man covered by a sheet was wheeled by just as Billy entered the corridor. The man had been a famous marathon runner in his day. So it goes. This was before Billy had his head broken in an airplane crash, by the way—before he became so vocal about flying saucers and traveling in time.

Billy sat down in a waiting room. He wasn't a widower yet. He sensed something hard under the cushion of his overstuffed chair. He dug it out, discovered that it was a book, *The Execution of Private Slovik,* by William Bradford Huie. It was a true account of the death before an American firing squad of Private Eddie D. Slovik, 36896415, the only American soldier to be shot for cowardice since the Civil War. So it goes.

Billy read the opinion of a staff judge advocate who reviewed Slovik's case, which ended like this: *He has directly challenged the authority of the government, and future discipline depends upon a resolute reply to this challenge. If the death penalty is ever to be imposed for desertion, it should be imposed in this case, not as a punitive measure nor as retribution, but to maintain that discipline upon which alone an army can succeed against the enemy. There was no recommendation for clemency in the case and none is here recommended.* So it goes.

Billy blinked in 1965, traveled in time to 1958. He was at a banquet in honor of a Little League team of which his son Robert was a member. The coach, who had never been married, was speaking. He was all choked up. "Honest to God," he was saying, "I'd consider it an honor just to be *water* boy for these kids."

Billy blinked in 1958, traveled in time to 1961. It was New Year's Eve, and Billy was disgracefully drunk at a party where everybody was in optometry or married to an optometrist.

Billy usually didn't drink much, because the war had ruined his stomach, but he certainly had a snootful now, and he was being unfaithful to his wife Valencia for the first and only time. He had somehow persuaded a woman to come into the laundry room of the house, and then sit up on the gas dryer, which was running.

The woman was very drunk herself, and she helped Billy get her girdle off. "What was it you wanted to talk about?" she said.

"It's all right," said Billy. He honestly thought it was all right. He couldn't remember the name of the woman.

"How come they call you Billy instead of William?"

"Business reasons," said Billy. That was true. His father-in-law, who owned the Ilium School of Optometry, who had set Billy up in practice, was a genius in his field. He told Billy to encourage people to call him Billy—because it would stick in their memories. It would also make him seem slightly magical, since there weren't any other grown Billys around. It also compelled people to think of him as a friend right away.

Somewhere in there was an awful scene, with people expressing disgust for Billy and the woman, and Billy found himself out in his automobile, trying to find the steering wheel.

The main thing now was to find the steering wheel. At first, Billy windmilled his arms, hoping to find it by luck. When that didn't work, he became methodical, working in such a way that the wheel could not possibly escape him. He placed himself hard against the left-hand door, searched every square inch of the area before him. When he failed to find the wheel, he moved over six inches, and searched again. Amazingly, he was eventually hard against the right-hand door, without having found the wheel. He concluded that somebody had stolen it. This angered him as he passed out.

He was in the back seat of his car, which was why he couldn't find the steering wheel.

Now somebody was shaking Billy awake. Billy still felt drunk, was still angered by the stolen steering wheel. He was back in World War Two again, behind the German lines. The person who was shaking him was Roland Weary. Weary had gathered the front of Billy's field jacket into his hands. He banged Billy against a tree, then pulled him away from it, flung him in the direction he was supposed to take under his own power.

Billy stopped, shook his head. "You go on," he said.

"What?"

"You guys go on without me. I'm all right."

"You're what?"

"I'm O.K."

"Jesus—I'd hate to see somebody *sick*," said Weary, through five layers of humid scarf from home. Billy had never seen Weary's face. He had tried to imagine it one time, had imaged a toad in a fishbowl.

Weary kicked and shoved Billy for a quarter of a mile. The scouts were waiting between the banks of a frozen creek. They had heard the dog. They had heard men calling back and forth, too—calling like hunters who had a pretty good idea of where their quarry was.

The banks of the creek were high enough to allow the scouts to stand without being seen. Billy staggered down the bank ridiculously. After him came Weary, clanking and clinking and tinkling and hot.

[41]

"Here he is, boys," said Weary. "He don't want to live, but he's gonna live anyway. When he gets out of this, by God, he's gonna owe his life to the Three Musketeers." This was the first the scouts had heard that Weary thought of himself and them as the Three Musketeers.

Billy Pilgrim, there in the creekbed, thought he, Billy Pilgrim, was turning to steam painlessly. If everybody would leave him alone for just a little while, he thought, he wouldn't cause anybody any more trouble. He would turn to steam and float up among the treetops.

Somewhere the big dog barked again. With the help of fear and echoes and winter silences, that dog had a voice like a big bronze gong.

Roland Weary, eighteen years old, insinuated himself between the scouts, draped a heavy arm around the shoulder of each. "So what do the Three Musketeers do now?" he said.

Billy Pilgrim was having a delightful hallucination. He was wearing dry, warm, white sweatsocks, and he was skating on a ballroom floor. Thousands cheered. This wasn't time-travel. It had never happened, never would happen. It was the craziness of a dying young man with his shoes full of snow.

One scout hung his head, let spit fall from his lips. The other did the same. They studied the infinitesimal effects of spit on snow and history. They were small, graceful people. They had been behind German lines before many times—living like woods creatures, living from moment to moment in useful terror, thinking brainlessly with their spinal cords.

Now they twisted out from under Weary's loving arms. They told Weary that he and Billy had better find somebody to surrender to. The scouts weren't going to wait for them any more.

And they ditched Weary and Billy in the creekbed.

Billy Pilgrim went on skating, doing tricks in sweat-socks, tricks that most people would consider impossible—making turns, stopping on a dime and so on. The cheering went on, but its tone was altered as the hallucination gave way to time-travel.

Billy stopped skating, found himself at a lectern in a Chinese restaurant in Ilium, New York, on an early afternoon in the autumn of 1957. He was receiving a standing ovation from the Lions Club. He had just been elected President, and it was necessary that he speak. He was scared stiff, thought a ghastly mistake had been made. All those prosperous, solid men out there would discover now that they had elected a ludicrous waif. They would hear his reedy voice, the one he'd had in the war. He swallowed, knew that all he had for a voice box was a little whistle cut from a willow switch. Worse—he had nothing to say. The crowd quieted down. Everybody was pink and beaming.

Billy opened his mouth, and out came a deep, resonant tone. His voice was a gorgeous instrument. It told jokes which brought down the house. It grew serious, told jokes again, and ended on a note of humility. The explanation of the miracle was this: Billy had taken a course in public speaking.

And then he was back in the bed of the frozen creek again. Roland Weary was about to beat the living shit out of him.

Weary was filled with a tragic wrath. He had been ditched again. He stuffed his pistol into its holster. He slipped his knife into its scabbard. Its triangular blade and blood gutters on all three faces. And then he shook Billy hard, rattled his skeleton, slammed him against a bank.

Weary barked and whimpered through his layers of scarf from home. He spoke unintelligibly of the sacrifices he had made on Billy's behalf. He dilated upon the piety and heroism of "The Three Musketeers," portrayed, in the most glowing and impassioned hues, their virtue and magnanimity, the imperishable honor they acquired for themselves, and the great services they rendered to Christianity.

It was entirely Billy's fault that this fighting organization no longer existed, Weary felt, and Billy was going to pay. Weary socked Billy a good one on the side of his jaw, knocked Billy away from the bank and onto the snow-covered ice of the creek. Billy was down on all fours on the ice, and Weary kicked him in the ribs, rolled him over on his side. Billy tried to form himself into a ball.

"You shouldn't even *be* in the Army," said Weary.

Billy was involuntarily making convulsive sounds that were a lot like laughter. "You think it's funny, huh?" Weary inquired. He walked around to Billy's back. Billy's jacket and shirt and undershirt had been hauled up around his shoulders by the violence, so his back was naked. There, inches from the tips of Weary's combat boots, were the pitiful buttons of Billy's spine.

Weary drew back his right boot, aimed a kick at the spine, at the tube which had so many of Billy's important wires in it. Weary was going to break that tube.

But then Weary saw that he had an audience. Five German soldiers and a police dog on a leash were looking down into the bed of the creek. The soldiers' blue eyes were filled with a bleary civilian curiosity as to why one American would try to murder another one so far from home, and why the victim should laugh.

[44]

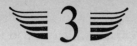

3

The Germans and the dog were engaged in a military operation which had an amusingly self-explanatory name, a human enterprise which is seldom described in detail, whose name alone, when reported as news or history, gives many war enthusiasts a sort of post-coital satisfaction. It is, in the imagination of combat's fans, the divinely listless loveplay that follows the orgasm of victory. It is called "mopping up."

The dog, who had sounded so ferocious in the winter distances, was a female German shepherd. She was shivering. Her tail was between her legs. She had been borrowed that morning from a farmer. She had never been to war before. She had no idea what game was being played. Her name was Princess.

Two of the Germans were boys in their early teens. Two were ramshackle old men—droolers as toothless as carp. They were irregulars, armed and clothed fragmentarily with junk taken from real soldiers who were newly dead. So it goes. They were farmers from just across the German border, not far away.

Their commander was a middle-aged corporal—red-eyed, scrawny, tough as dried beef, sick of war. He had been wounded four times—and patched up, and sent back to war. He was a very good soldier—about to quit, about to find somebody to surrender to. His bandy legs were thrust into golden cavalry boots which he had taken from a dead Hungarian colonel on the Russian front. So it goes.

Those boots were almost all he owned in this world. They were his home. An anecdote: One time a recruit was watching him bone and wax those golden boots, and he held one up to the recruit and said, "If you look in there deeply enough, you'll see Adam and Eve."

Billy Pilgrim had not heard this anecdote. But, lying on the black ice there, Billy stared into the patina of the corporal's boots, saw Adam and Eve in the golden depths. They were naked. They were so innocent, so vulnerable, so eager to behave decently. Billy Pilgrim loved them.

Next to the golden boots were a pair of feet which were swaddled in rags. They were crisscrossed by canvas straps, were shod with hinged wooden clogs. Billy looked up at the face that went with the clogs. It was the face of a blond angel, of a fifteen-year-old boy.

The boy was as beautiful as Eve.

Billy was helped to his feet by the lovely boy, by the heavenly androgyne. And the others came forward to dust the snow off Billy, and then they searched him for weapons. He didn't have any. The most dangerous thing they found on his person was a two-inch pencil stub.

Three inoffensive *bangs* came from far away. They came from German rifles. The two scouts who had ditched Billy and Weary had just been shot. They had been lying in ambush for Germans. They had been discovered and shot from behind. Now they were dying in the snow, feeling nothing, turning the snow to the color of raspberry sherbet. So it goes. So Roland Weary was the last of the Three Musketeers.

And Weary, bug-eyed with terror, was being disarmed. The corporal gave Weary's pistol to the pretty boy. He marveled at Weary's cruel trench knife, said in German that Weary would no doubt like to use the knife on him, to tear his face off with the spiked knuckles, to stick the blade into his belly or throat. He spoke no English, and Billy and Weary understood no German.

"Nice playthings you have," the corporal told Weary, and he handed the knife to an old man. "Isn't that a pretty thing? Hmmm?"

He tore open Weary's overcoat and blouse. Brass buttons flew like popcorn. The corporal reached into Weary's gaping bosom as though he meant to tear out his pounding heart, but he brought out Weary's bullet-proof Bible instead.

A bullet-proof Bible is a Bible small enough to be slipped into a soldier's breast pocket, over his heart. It is sheathed in steel.

The corporal found the dirty picture of the woman and the pony in Weary's hip pocket. "What a lucky pony, eh?" he said. "Hmmmm? Hmmmm? Don't you wish you were that pony?" He handed the picture to the other old man. "Spoils of war! It's yours, all yours, you lucky lad."

Then he made Weary sit down in the snow and take off his combat boots, which he gave to the beautiful boy. He gave Weary the boy's clogs. So Weary and Billy were both without decent military footwear now, and they had to walk for miles and miles, with Weary's clogs clacking, with Billy bobbing up-and-down, up-and-down, crashing into Weary from time to time.

"Excuse me," Billy would say, or "I beg your pardon."

They were brought at last to a stone cottage at a fork in the road. It was a collecting point for prisoners of war. Billy and Weary were taken inside, where it was warm and smoky. There was a fire sizzling and popping in the fireplace. The fuel was furniture. There were about twenty other Americans in there, sitting on the floor with their backs to the wall, staring into the flames—thinking whatever there was to think, which was zero.

Nobody talked. Nobody had any good war stories to tell.

Billy and Weary found places for themselves, and Billy went to sleep with his head on the shoulder of an unprotesting captain. The captain was a chaplain. He was a rabbi. He had been shot through the hand.

Billy traveled in time, opened his eyes, found himself staring into the glass eyes of a jade green mechanical owl. The owl was hanging upside down from a rod of stainless steel. The owl was Billy's optometer in his office in Ilium. An optometer is an instrument for measuring refractive errors in eyes—in order that corrective lenses may be prescribed.

Billy had fallen asleep while examining a female patient who was in a chair on the other side of the owl. He had fallen asleep at work before. It had been funny at first. Now Billy was starting to get worried about it, about his mind in general. He tried to remember how old he was, couldn't. He tried to remember what year it was. He couldn't remember that, either.

"Doctor—" said the patient tentatively.

"Hm?" he said.

"You're so quiet."

"Sorry."

"You were talking away there—and then you got so quiet."

"Um."

"You see something terrible?"

"Terrible?"

"Some disease in my eyes?"

"No, no," said Billy, wanting to doze again. "Your eyes are fine. You just need glasses for reading." He told her to go across the corridor—to see the wide selection of frames there.

When she was gone, Billy opened the drapes and was no wiser as to what was outside. The view was still blocked by a venetian blind, which he hoisted clatteringly. Bright sunlight came crashing in. There were thousands of parked automobiles out there, twinkling on a vast lake of blacktop. Billy's office was part of a suburban shopping center.

Right outside the window was Billy's own Cadillac El Dorado Coupe de Ville. He read the stickers on the bumper. "Visit Ausable Chasm," said one. "Support Your Police Department," said another. There was a third. "Impeach Earl Warren," it said. The stickers about the police and Earl Warren were gifts from Billy's father-in-law, a member of the John Birch Society. The date on the license plate was 1967, which would make Billy Pilgrim forty-four years old. He asked himself this: "Where have all the years gone?"

Billy turned his attention to his desk. There was an open copy of *The Review of Optometry* there. It was opened to an editorial, which Billy now read, his lips moving slightly.

What happens in 1968 will rule the fate of European optometrists for at least 50 years! Billy read. *With this warning, Jean Thiriart, Secretary of the National Union of Belgium Opticians, is pressing for formation of a "European Optometry Society." The alternatives, he says, will be the obtaining of professional status, or, by 1971, reduction to the role of spectacle-sellers.*

Billy Pilgrim tried hard to care.

A siren went off, scared the hell out of him. He was expecting World War Three at any time. The siren was simply announcing high noon. It was housed in a cupola atop a firehouse across the street from Billy's office.

Billy closed his eyes. When he opened them, he was back in World War Two again. His head was on the wounded rabbi's shoulder. A German was kicking his feet, telling him to wake up, that it was time to move on.

The Americans, with Billy among them, formed a fools' parade on the road outside.

There was a photographer present, a German war correspondent with a Leica. He took pictures of Billy's and Roland Weary's feet. The picture was widely published two days later as heartening evidence of how miserably equipped the American Army often was, despite its reputation for being rich.

The photographer wanted something more lively, though, a picture of an actual capture. So the guards staged one for him. They threw Billy into shrubbery. When Billy came out of the shrubbery, his face wreathed in goofy good will, they menaced him with their machine pistols, as though they were capturing him then.

Billy's smile as he came out of the shrubbery was at least as peculiar as Mona Lisa's, for he was simultaneously on foot in Germany in 1944 and riding his Cadillac in 1967. Germany dropped away, and 1967 became bright and clear, free of interference from any other time. Billy was on his way to a Lions Club luncheon meeting. It was a hot August, but Billy's car was air-conditioned. He was stopped by a signal in the middle of Ilium's black ghetto. The people who lived here hated it so much that they had burned down a lot of it a month before. It was all they had, and they'd wrecked it. The neighborhood reminded Billy of some of the towns he had seen in the war. The curbs and sidewalks were crushed in many places, showing where the National Guard tanks and half-tracks had been.

"Blood brother," said a message written in pink paint on the side of a shattered grocery store.

There was a tap on Billy's car window. A black man was out there. He wanted to talk about something. The light had changed. Billy did the simplest thing. He drove on.

Billy drove through a scene of even greater desolation. It looked like Dresden after it was fire-bombed—like the surface of the moon. The house where Billy had grown up used to be somewhere in what was so empty now. This was urban renewal. A new Ilium Government Center and a Pavilion of the Arts and a Peace Lagoon and high-rise apartment buildings were going up here soon.

That was all right with Billy Pilgrim.

The speaker at the Lions Club meeting was a major in the Marines. He said that Americans had no choice but to keep fighting in Vietnam until they achieved victory or until the Communists realized that they could not force their way of life on weak countries. The major had been there on two separate tours of duty. He told of many terrible and many wonderful things he had seen. He was in favor of increased bombings, of bombing North Vietnam back into the Stone Age, if it refused to see reason.

Billy was not moved to protest the bombing of North Vietnam, did not shudder about the hideous things he himself had seen bombing do. He was simply having lunch with the Lions Club, of which he was past president now.

Billy had a framed prayer on his office wall which expressed his method for keeping going, even though he was unenthusiastic about living. A lot of patients who saw the prayer on Billy's wall told him that it helped *them* to keep going, too. It went like this:

GOD GRANT ME
THE SERENITY TO ACCEPT
THE THINGS I CANNOT CHANGE,
COURAGE
TO CHANGE THE THINGS I CAN,
AND WISDOM ALWAYS
TO TELL THE
DIFFERENCE.

Among the things Billy Pilgrim could not change were the past, the present, and the future.

Now he was being introduced to the Marine major. The person who was performing the introduction was telling the major that Billy was a veteran, and that Billy had a son who was a sergeant in the Green Berets—in Vietnam.

The major told Billy that the Green Berets were doing a great job, and that he should be proud of his son.

"I *am*. I certainly *am*," said Billy Pilgrim.

He went home for a nap after lunch. He was under doctor's orders to take a nap every day. The doctor hoped that this would relieve a complaint that Billy had: Every so often, for no apparent reason, Billy Pilgrim would find himself weeping. Nobody had ever caught Billy doing it. Only the doctor knew. It was an extremely quiet thing Billy did, and not very moist.

Billy owned a lovely Georgian home in Ilium. He was rich as Croesus, something he had never expected to be, not in a million years. He had five other optometrists working for him in the shopping plaza location, and netted over sixty thousand dollars a year. In addition, he owned a fifth of the new Holiday Inn out on Route 54, and half of three Tastee-Freeze stands. Tastee-Freeze was a sort of frozen custard. It gave all the pleasure that ice cream could give, without the stiffness and bitter coldness of ice cream.

Billy's home was empty. His daughter Barbara was about to get married, and she and his wife had gone downtown to pick out patterns for her crystal and silverware. There was a note saying so on the kitchen table. There were no servants. People just weren't interested in careers in domestic service anymore. There wasn't a dog, either.

There used to be a dog named Spot, but he died. So it goes. Billy had liked Spot a lot, and Spot had liked him.

Billy went up the carpeted stairway and into his and his wife's bedroom. The room had flowered wallpaper. There was a double bed with a clock-radio on a table beside it. Also on the table were controls for the electric blanket, and a switch to turn on a gentle vibrator which was bolted to the springs of the box mattress. The trade name of the vibrator was "Magic Fingers." The vibrator was the doctor's idea, too.

Billy took off his tri-focals and his coat and his necktie and his shoes, and he closed the venetian blinds and then the drapes, and he lay down on the outside of the coverlet. But sleep would not come. Tears came instead. They seeped. Billy turned on the Magic Fingers, and he was jiggled as he wept.

The doorchimes rang. Billy got off the bed and looked down through a window at the front doorstep, to see if somebody important had come to call. There was a crippled man down there, as spastic in space as Billy Pilgrim was in time. Convulsions made the man dance flappingly all the time, made him change his expressions, too, as though he were trying to imitate various famous movie stars.

Another cripple was ringing a doorbell across the street. He was on crutches. He had only one leg. He was so jammed between his crutches that his shoulders hid his ears.

Billy knew what the cripples were up to: They were selling subscriptions to magazines that would never come. People subscribed to them because the salesmen were so pitiful. Billy had heard about this racket from a speaker at the Lions Club two weeks before—a man from the Better Business Bureau. The man said that anybody who saw cripples working a neighborhood for magazine subscriptions should call the police.

Billy looked down the street, saw a new Buick Riviera parked about half a block away. There was a man in it, and Billy assumed correctly that he was the man who had hired the cripples to do this thing. Billy went on weeping as he contemplated the cripples and their boss. His doorchimes clanged hellishly.

He closed his eyes, and opened them again. He was still weeping, but he was back in Luxembourg again. He was marching with a lot of other prisoners. It was a winter wind that was bringing tears to his eyes.

Ever since Billy had been thrown into shrubbery for the sake of a picture, he had been seeing Saint Elmo's fire, a sort of electronic radiance around the heads of his companions and captors. It was in the treetops and on the rooftops of Luxembourg, too. It was beautiful.

Billy was marching with his hands on top of his head, and so were all the other Americans. Billy was bobbing up-and-down, up-and-down. Now he crashed into Roland Weary accidentally. "I beg your pardon," he said.

Weary's eyes were tearful also. Weary was crying because of horrible pains in his feet. The hinged clogs were transforming his feet into blood puddings.

At each road intersection Billy's group was joined by more Americans with their hands on top of their haloed heads. Billy had smiles for them all. They were moving like water, downhill all the time, and they flowed at last to a main highway on a valley's floor. Through the valley flowed a Mississippi of humiliated Americans. Tens of thousands of Americans shuffled eastward, their hands clasped on top of their heads. They sighed and groaned.

Billy and his group joined the river of humiliation, and the late afternoon sun came out from the clouds. The Americans didn't have the road to themselves. The westbound lane boiled and boomed with vehicles which were rushing German reserves to the front. The reserves were violent, windburned, bristly men. They had teeth like piano keys.

[55]

They were festooned with machine-gun belts, smoked cigars and guzzled booze. They took wolfish bites from sausages, patted their horny palms with potato-masher grenades.

One soldier in black was having a drunk hero's picnic all by himself on top of a tank. He spit on the Americans. The spit hit Roland Weary's shoulder, gave Weary a *fourragère* of snot and blutwurst and tobacco juice and Schnapps.

Billy found the afternoon stingingly exciting. There was so much to see—dragon's teeth, killing machines, corpses with bare feet that were blue and ivory. So it goes.

Bobbing up-and-down, up-and-down, Billy beamed lovingly at a bright lavender farmhouse that had been spattered with machine-gun bullets. Standing in its cock-eyed doorway was a German colonel. With him was his unpainted whore.

Billy crashed into Weary's shoulder, and Weary cried out sobbingly. "Walk right! Walk right!"

They were climbing a gentle rise now. When they reached the top, they weren't in Luxembourg any more. They were in Germany.

A motion-picture camera was set up at the border—to record the fabulous victory. Two civilians in bearskin coats were leaning on the camera when Billy and Weary came by. They had run out of film hours ago.

One of them singled out Billy's face for a moment, then focused at infinity again. There was a tiny plume of smoke at infinity. There was a battle there. People were dying there. So it goes.

And the sun went down, and Billy found himself bobbing in place in a railroad yard. There were rows and rows of boxcars waiting. They had brought reserves to the front. Now they were going to take prisoners into Germany's interior.

Flashlight beams danced crazily.

The Germans sorted out the prisoners according to rank. They put sergeants with sergeants, majors with majors, and so on. A squad of full colonels was halted near Billy. One of them had double pneumonia. He had a high fever and vertigo. As the railroad yard dipped and swooped around the colonel, he tried to hold himself steady by staring into Billy's eyes.

The colonel coughed and coughed, and then he said to Billy, "You one of my boys?" This was a man who had lost an entire regiment, about forty-five hundred men—a lot of them children, actually. Billy didn't reply. The question made no sense.

"What was your outfit?" said the colonel. He coughed and coughed. Every time he inhaled his lungs rattled like greasy paper bags.

Billy couldn't remember the outfit he was from.

"You from the Four-fifty-first?"

"Four-fifty-first what?" said Billy.

There was a silence. "Infantry regiment," said the colonel at last.

"Oh," said Billy Pilgrim.

There was another long silence, with the colonel dying and dying, drowning where he stood. And then he cried out wetly, "It's me, boys! It's Wild Bob!" That is what he had always wanted his troops to call him: "Wild Bob."

None of the people who could hear him were actually from his regiment, except for Roland Weary, and Weary wasn't listening. All Weary could think of was the agony in his own feet.

But the colonel imagined that he was addressing his beloved troops for the last time, and he told them that they had nothing to be ashamed of, that there were dead Germans all over the battlefield who wished to God that they had never heard of the Four-fifty-first. He said that after the war he was going to have a regimental reunion in his home town, which was Cody, Wyoming. He was going to barbecue whole steers.

He said all this while staring into Billy's eyes. He made the inside of poor Billy's skull echo with balderdash. "God be with you, boys!" he said, and that echoed and echoed. And then he said, "If you're ever in Cody, Wyoming, just ask for Wild Bob!"

I was there. So was my old war buddy, Bernard V. O'Hare.

Billy Pilgrim was packed into a boxcar with many other privates. He and Roland Weary were separated. Weary was packed into another car in the same train.

There were narrow ventilators at the corners of the car, under the eaves. Billy stood by one of these, and, as the crowd pressed against him, he climbed part way up a diagonal corner brace to make more room. This placed his eyes on a level with the ventilator, so he could see another train about ten yards away.

Germans were writing on the cars with blue chalk—the number of persons in each car, their rank, their national-ity, the date on which they had been put aboard. Other Germans were securing the hasps on the car doors with wire and spikes and other trackside trash. Billy could hear

[58]

somebody writing on his car, too, but he couldn't see who was doing it.

Most of the privates on Billy's car were very young—at the end of childhood. But crammed into the corner with Billy was a former hobo who was forty years old.

"I been hungrier than this," the hobo told Billy. "I been in worse places than this. This ain't so bad."

A man in a boxcar across the way called out through the ventilator that a man had just died in there. So it goes. There were four guards who heard him. They weren't excited by the news.

"Yo, yo," said one, nodding dreamily. "Yo, yo."

And the guards didn't open the car with the dead man in it. They opened the next car instead, and Billy Pilgrim was enchanted by what was in there. It was like heaven. There was candlelight, and there were bunks with quilts and blankets heaped on them. There was a cannonball stove with a steaming coffeepot on top. There was a table with a bottle of wine and a loaf of bread and a sausage on it. There were four bowls of soup.

There were pictures of castles and lakes and pretty girls on the walls. This was the rolling home of the railroad guards, men whose business it was to be forever guarding freight rolling from here to there. The four guards went inside and closed the door.

A little while later they came out smoking cigars, talking contentedly in the mellow lower register of the German language. One of them saw Billy's face at the ventilator. He wagged a finger at him in affectionate warning, telling him to be a good boy.

The Americans across the way told the guards again about the dead man on their car. The guards got a stretcher out of their own cozy car, opened the dead man's car and went inside. The dead man's car wasn't crowded at all. There were just six live colonels in there—and one dead one.

The Germans carried the corpse out. The corpse was Wild Bob. So it goes.

During the night, some of the locomotives began to tootle to one another, and then to move. The locomotive and the last car of each train were marked with a striped banner of orange and black, indicating that the train was not fair game for airplanes—that it was carrying prisoners of war.

The war was nearly over. The locomotives began to move east in late December. The war would end in May. German prisons everywhere were absolutely full, and there was no longer any food for the prisoners to eat, and no longer any fuel to keep them warm. And yet—here came more prisoners.

Billy Pilgrim's train, the longest train of all, did not move for two days.

"This ain't bad," the hobo told Billy on the second day. "This ain't nothing at all."

Billy looked out through the ventilator. The railroad yard was a desert now, except for a hospital train marked with red crosses—on a siding far, far away. Its locomotive whistled. The locomotive of Billy Pilgrim's train whistled back. They were saying, "Hello."

Even though Billy's train wasn't moving, its boxcars were kept locked tight. Nobody was to get off until the final destination. To the guards who walked up and down outside, each car became a single organism which ate and drank and excreted through its ventilators. It talked or sometimes yelled through its ventilators, too. In went water and loaves of blackbread and sausage and cheese, and out came shit and piss and language.

Human beings in there were excreting into steel helmets, which were passed to the people at the ventilators, who dumped them. Billy was a dumper. The human beings also passed canteens, which guards would fill with water. When food came in, the human beings were quiet and trusting and beautiful. They shared.

Human beings in there took turns standing or lying down. The legs of those who stood were like fence posts driven into a warm, squirming, farting, sighing earth. The queer earth was a mosaic of sleepers who nestled like spoons.

Now the train began to creep eastward.

Somewhere in there was Christmas. Billy Pilgrim nestled like a spoon with the hobo on Christmas night, and he fell asleep, and he traveled in time to 1967 again—to the night he was kidnapped by a flying saucer from Tralfamadore.

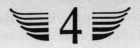

4

Billy Pilgrim could not sleep on his daughter's wedding night. He was forty-four. The wedding had taken place that afternoon in a gaily striped tent in Billy's backyard. The stripes were orange and black.

Billy and his wife, Valencia, nestled like spoons in their big double bed. They were jiggled by Magic Fingers. Valencia didn't need to be jiggled to sleep. Valencia was snoring like a bandsaw. The poor woman didn't have ovaries or a uterus any more. They had been removed by a surgeon—by one of Billy's partners in the new Holiday Inn.

There was a full moon.

Billy got out of bed in the moonlight. He felt spooky and luminous, felt as though he were wrapped in cool fur that was full of static electricity. He looked down at his bare feet. They were ivory and blue.

Billy now shuffled down his upstairs hallway, knowing he was about to be kidnapped by a flying saucer. The hallway was zebra-striped with darkness and moonlight. The moonlight came into the hallway through doorways of the empty rooms of Billy's two children, children no more. They were gone forever. Billy was guided by dread and the lack of dread. Dread told him when to stop. Lack of it told him when to move again. He stopped.

He went into his daughter's room. Her drawers were dumped. Her closet was empty. Heaped in the middle of the room were all the possessions she could not take on a honeymoon. She had a Princess telephone extension all her own—on her windowsill. Its tiny night light stared at Billy. And then it rang.

Billy answered. There was a drunk on the other end. Billy could almost smell his breath—mustard gas and roses. It was a wrong number. Billy hung up. There was a soft drink bottle on the windowsill. Its label boasted that it contained no nourishment whatsoever.

Billy Pilgrim padded downstairs on his blue and ivory feet. He went into the kitchen, where the moonlight called his attention to a half bottle of champagne on the kitchen table, all that was left from the reception in the tent. Somebody had stoppered it again. "Drink me," it seemed to say.

So Billy uncorked it with his thumbs. It didn't make a pop. The champagne was dead. So it goes.

Billy looked at the clock on the gas stove. He had an hour to kill before the saucer came. He went into the living room, swinging the bottle like a dinner bell, turned on the television. He came slightly unstuck in time, saw the late movie backwards, then forwards again. It was a movie about American bombers in the Second World War and the gallant men who flew them. Seen backwards by Billy, the story went like this:

American planes, full of holes and wounded men and corpses took off backwards from an airfield in England.

Over France, a few German fighter planes flew at them backwards, sucked bullets and shell fragments from some of the planes and crewmen. They did the same for wrecked American bombers on the ground, and those planes flew up backwards to join the formation.

The formation flew backwards over a German city that was in flames. The bombers opened their bomb bay doors, exerted a miraculous magnetism which shrunk the fires, gathered them into cylindrical steel containers, and lifted the containers into the bellies of the planes. The containers were stored neatly in racks. The Germans below had miraculous devices of their own, which were long steel tubes. They used them to suck more fragments from the crewmen and planes. But there were still a few wounded Americans, though, and some of the bombers were in bad repair. Over France, though, German fighters came up again, made everything and everybody as good as new.

When the bombers got back to their base, the steel cylinders were taken from the racks and shipped back to the United States of America, where factories were operating night and day, dismantling the cylinders, separating the dangerous contents into minerals. Touchingly, it was mainly women who did this work. The minerals were then shipped to specialists in remote areas. It was their business to put them into the ground, to hide them cleverly, so they would never hurt anybody ever again.

The American fliers turned in their uniforms, became high school kids. And Hitler turned into a baby, Billy Pilgrim supposed. That wasn't in the movie. Billy was extrapolating. Everybody turned into a baby, and all humanity, without exception, conspired biologically to produce two perfect people named Adam and Eve, he supposed.

Billy saw the war movies backwards then forwards—and then it was time to go out into his backyard to meet the flying saucer. Out he went, his blue and ivory feet crushing the wet salad of the lawn. He stopped, took a swig of the dead champagne. It was like 7-Up. He would not raise his eyes to the sky, though he knew there was a flying saucer from Tralfamadore up there. He would see it soon enough, inside and out, and he would see, too, where it came from soon enough—soon enough.

Overhead he heard the cry of what might have been a melodious owl, but it wasn't a melodious owl. It was a flying saucer from Tralfamadore, navigating in both space and time, therefore seeming to Billy Pilgrim to have come from nowhere all at once. Somewhere a big dog barked.

The saucer was one hundred feet in diameter, with portholes around its rim. The light from the portholes was a pulsing purple. The only noise it made was the owl song. It came down to hover over Billy, and to enclose him in a cylinder of pulsing purple light. Now there was the sound of a seeming kiss as an airtight hatch in the bottom of the saucer was opened. Down snaked a ladder that was outlined in pretty lights like a Ferris wheel.

Billy's will was paralyzed by a zap gun aimed at him from one of the portholes. It became imperative that he take hold of the bottom rung of the sinuous ladder, which he did. The rung was electrified, so that Billy's hands locked onto it hard. He was hauled into the airlock, and machinery closed the bottom door. Only then did the ladder, wound onto a reel in the airlock, let him go. Only then did Billy's brain start working again.

There were two peepholes inside the airlock—with yellow eyes pressed to them. There was a speaker on the wall. The Tralfamadorians had no voice boxes. They communicated telepathically. They were able to talk to Billy by means of a computer and a sort of electric organ which made every Earthling speech sound.

"Welcome aboard, Mr. Pilgrim," said the loudspeaker. "Any questions?"

Billy licked his lips, thought a while, inquired at last: "Why me?"

"That is a very *Earthling* question to ask, Mr. Pilgrim. Why *you?* Why *us* for that matter? Why *anything?* Because this moment simply *is.* Have you ever seen bugs trapped in amber?"

"Yes." Billy, in fact, had a paperweight in his office which was a blob of polished amber with three ladybugs embedded in it.

"Well, here we are, Mr. Pilgrim, trapped in the amber of this moment. There is no *why.*"

They introduced an anesthetic into Billy's atmosphere now, put him to sleep. They carried him to a cabin where he was strapped to a yellow Barca-Lounger which they had stolen from a Sears & Roebuck warehouse. The hold of the saucer was crammed with other stolen merchandise, which would be used to furnish Billy's artificial habitat in a zoo on Tralfamadore.

The terrific acceleration of the saucer as it left Earth twisted Billy's slumbering body, distorted his face, dislodged him in time, sent him back to the war.

[66]

When he regained consciousness, he wasn't on the flying saucer. He was in a boxcar crossing Germany again.

Some people were rising from the floor of the car, and others were lying down. Billy planned to lie down, too. It would be lovely to sleep. It was black in the car, and black outside the car, which seemed to be going about two miles an hour. The car never seemed to go any faster than that. It was a long time between clicks, between joints in the track. There would be a click, and then a year would go by, and then there would be another click.

The train often stopped to let really important trains bawl and hurtle by. Another thing it did was stop on sidings near prisons, leaving a few cars there. It was creeping across all of Germany, growing shorter all the time.

And Billy let himself down oh so gradually now, hanging onto the diagonal cross-brace in the corner in order to make himself seem nearly weightless to those he was joining on the floor. He knew it was important that he make himself nearly ghostlike when lying down. He had forgotten why, but a reminder soon came.

"Pilgrim—" said a person he was about to nestle with, "is that *you?*"

Billy didn't say anything, but nestled very politely, closed his eyes.

"God damn it," said the person. "That *is* you, isn't it?" He sat up and explored Billy rudely with his hands. "It's you, all right. Get the hell out of here."

Now Billy sat up, too—wretched, close to tears.

"Get out of here! I want to sleep!"

"Shut up," said somebody else.

"I'll shut up when Pilgrim gets away from here."

So Billy stood up again, clung to the cross-brace. "Where *can* I sleep?" he asked quietly.

"Not with me."

"Not with me, you son of a bitch," said somebody else. "You yell. You kick."

"I do?"

"You're God damn right you do. And whimper."

"I do?"

"Keep the hell away from here, Pilgrim."

And now there was an acrimonious madrigal, with parts sung in all quarters of the car. Nearly everybody, seemingly, had an atrocity story of something Billy Pilgrim had done to him in his sleep. Everybody told Billy Pilgrim to keep the hell away.

So Billy Pilgrim had to sleep standing up, or not sleep at all. And food had stopped coming in through the ventilators, and the days and nights were colder all the time.

On the eighth day, the forty-year-old hobo said to Billy, "This ain't bad. I can be comfortable anywhere."

"You can?" said Billy.

On the ninth day, the hobo died. So it goes. His last words were, "You think this is bad? This ain't bad."

There was something about death and the ninth day. There was a death on the ninth day in the car ahead of Billy's too. Roland Weary died—of gangrene that had started in his mangled feet. So it goes.

Weary, in his nearly continuous delirium, told again and again of the Three Musketeers, acknowledged that he was dying, gave many messages to be delivered to his family in Pittsburgh. Above all, he wanted to be avenged, so he said again and again the name of the person who had killed him. Everyone on the car learned the lesson well.

"Who killed me?" he would ask.

And everybody knew the answer, which was this: "Billy Pilgrim."

Listen—on the tenth night the peg was pulled out of the hasp on Billy's boxcar door, and the door was opened. Billy Pilgrim was lying at an angle on the corner-brace, self-crucified, holding himself there with a blue and ivory claw hooked over the sill of the ventilator. Billy coughed when the door was opened, and when he coughed he shit thin gruel. This was in accordance with the Third Law of Motion according to Sir Isaac Newton. This law tells us that for every action there is a reaction which is equal and opposite in direction.

This can be useful in rocketry.

The train had arrived on a siding by a prison which was originally constructed as an extermination camp for Russian prisoners of war.

The guards peeked inside Billy's car owlishly, cooed calmingly. They had never dealt with Americans before, but they surely understood this general sort of freight. They knew that it was essentially a liquid which could be induced to flow slowly toward cooing and light. It was nighttime.

The only light outside came from a single bulb which hung from a pole—high and far away. All was quiet outside, except for the guards, who cooed like doves. And the liquid began to flow. Gobs of it built up in the doorway, plopped to the ground.

Billy was the next-to-last human being to reach the door. The hobo was last. The hobo could not flow, could not plop. He wasn't liquid any more. He was stone. So it goes.

Billy didn't want to drop from the car to the ground. He sincerely believed that he would shatter like glass. So the guards helped him down, cooing still. They set him down facing the train. It was such a dinky train now.

There was a locomotive, a tender, and three little boxcars. The last boxcar was the railroad guards' heaven on wheels. Again—in that heaven on wheels—the table was set. Dinner was served.

At the base of the pole from which the light bulb hung were three seeming haystacks. The Americans were wheedled and teased over to those three stacks, which weren't hay after all. They were overcoats taken from prisoners who were dead. So it goes.

It was the guards' firmly expressed wish that every American without an overcoat should take one. The coats were cemented together with ice, so the guards used their bayonets as ice picks, pricking free collars and hems and sleeves and so on, then peeling off coats and handing them out at random. The coats were stiff and dome-shaped, having conformed to their piles.

The coat that Billy Pilgrim got had been crumpled and frozen in such a way, and was so small, that it appeared to be not a coat but a sort of large black, three-cornered hat. There were gummy stains on it, too, like crankcase drainings or old strawberry jam. There seemed to be a dead, furry animal frozen to it. The animal was in fact the coat's fur collar.

Billy glanced dully at the coats of his neighbors. Their coats all had brass buttons or tinsel or piping or numbers or stripes or eagles or moons or stars dangling from them. They were soldiers' coats. Billy was the only one who had a coat from a dead civilian. So it goes.

And Billy and the rest were encouraged to shuffle around their dinky train and into the prison camp. There wasn't anything warm or lively to attract them—merely long, low, narrow sheds by the thousands, with no lights inside.

Somewhere a dog barked. With the help of fear and echoes and winter silences, that dog had a voice like a big bronze gong.

Billy and the rest were wooed through gate after gate, and Billy saw his first Russian. The man was all alone in the night—a ragbag with a round, flat face that glowed like a radium dial.

Billy passed within a yard of him. There was barbed wire between them. The Russian did not wave or speak, but he looked directly into Billy's soul with sweet hopefulness, as though Billy might have good news for him—news he might be too stupid to understand, but good news all the same.

Billy blacked out as he walked through gate after gate. He came to in what he thought might be a building on Tralfamadore. It was shrilly lit and lined with white tiles. It was on Earth, though. It was a delousing station through which all new prisoners had to pass.

Billy did as he was told, took off his clothes. That was the first thing they told him to do on Tralfamadore, too.

A German measured Billy's upper right arm with his

thumb and forefinger, asked a companion what sort of an army would send a weakling like that to the front. They looked at the other American bodies now, pointed out a lot more that were nearly as bad as Billy's.

One of the best bodies belonged to the oldest American by far, a high school teacher from Indianapolis. His name was Edgar Derby. He hadn't been in Billy's boxcar. He'd been in Roland Weary's car, had cradled Weary's head while he died. So it goes. Derby was forty-four years old. He was so old he had a son who was a marine in the Pacific theater of war.

Derby had pulled political wires to get into the army at his age. The subject he had taught in Indianapolis was Contemporary Problems in Western Civilization. He also coached the tennis team, and took very good care of his body.

Derby's son would survive the war. Derby wouldn't. That good body of his would be filled with holes by a firing squad in Dresden in sixty-eight days. So it goes.

The worst American body wasn't Billy's. The worst body belonged to a car thief from Cicero, Illinois. His name was Paul Lazzaro. He was tiny, and not only were his bones and teeth rotten, but his skin was disgusting. Lazzaro was polka-dotted all over with dime-sized scars. He had had many plagues of boils.

Lazzaro, too, had been on Roland Weary's boxcar, and had given his word of honor to Weary that he would find some way to make Billy Pilgrim pay for Weary's death. He was looking around now, wondering which naked human being was Billy.

The naked Americans took their places under many showerheads along a white-tiled wall. There were no faucets they could control. They could only wait for whatever was coming. Their penises were shriveled and their balls were retracted. Reproduction was not the main business of the evening.

An unseen hand turned a master valve. Out of the showerheads gushed scalding rain. The rain was a blowtorch that did not warm. It jazzed and jangled Billy's skin without thawing the ice in the marrow of his long bones.

The Americans' clothes were meanwhile passing through poison gas. Body lice and bacteria and fleas were dying by the billions. So it goes.

And Billy zoomed back in time to his infancy. He was a baby who had just been bathed by his mother. Now his mother wrapped him in a towel, carried him into a rosy room that was filled with sunshine. She unwrapped him, laid him on the tickling towel, powdered him between his legs, joked with him, patted his little jelly belly. Her palm on his little jelly belly made potching sounds.

Billy gurgled and cooed.

And then Billy was a middle-aged optometrist again, playing hacker's golf this time—on a blazing summer Sunday morning. Billy never went to church any more. He was hacking with three other optometrists. Billy was on the green in seven strokes, and it was his turn to putt.

It was an eight-foot putt and he made it. He bent over to take the ball out of the cup, and the sun went behind a cloud. Billy was momentarily dizzy. When he recovered, he wasn't on the golf course any more. He was strapped to a yellow contour chair in a white chamber aboard a flying saucer, which was bound for Tralfamadore.

"Where am I?" said Billy Pilgrim.

"Trapped in another blob of amber, Mr. Pilgrim. We are where we have to be just now—three hundred million miles from Earth, bound for a time warp which will get us to Tralfamadore in hours rather than centuries."

"How—how did I get here?"

"It would take another Earthling to explain it to you. Earthlings are the great explainers, explaining why this event is structured as it is, telling how other events may be achieved or avoided. I am a Tralfamadorian, seeing all time as you might see a stretch of the Rocky Mountains. All time is all time. It does not change. It does not lend itself to warnings or explanations. It simply *is*. Take it moment by moment, and you will find that we are all, as I've said before, bugs in amber."

"You sound to me as though you don't believe in free will," said Billy Pilgrim.

"If I hadn't spent so much time studying Earthlings," said the Tralfamadorian, "I wouldn't have any idea what was meant by 'free will.' I've visited thirty-one inhabited planets in the universe, and I have studied reports on one hundred more. Only on Earth is there any talk of free will."

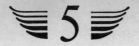

5

Billy Pilgrim says that the Universe does not look like a lot of bright little dots to the creatures from Tralfamadore. The creatures can see where each star has been and where it is going, so that the heavens are filled with rarefied, luminous spaghetti. And Tralfamadorians don't see human beings as two-legged creatures, either. They see them as great millepedes—"with babies' legs at one end and old people's legs at the other," says Billy Pilgrim.

Billy asked for something to read on the trip to Tralfamadore. His captors had five million Earthling books on microfilm, but no way to project them in Billy's cabin. They had only one actual book in English, which would be placed in a Tralfamadorian museum. It was *Valley of the Dolls*, by Jacqueline Susann.

Billy read it, thought it was pretty good in spots. The people in it certainly had their ups and downs, ups and downs. But Billy didn't want to read about the same ups and downs over and over again. He asked if there wasn't, please, some other reading matter around.

"Only Tralfamadorian novels, which I'm afraid you couldn't begin to understand," said the speaker on the wall.

"Let me look at one anyway."

So they sent him in several. They were little things. A dozen of them might have had the bulk of *Valley of the Dolls*—with all its ups and downs, ups and downs.

Billy couldn't read Tralfamadorian, of course, but he could at least see how the books were laid out—in brief clumps of symbols separated by stars. Billy commented that the clumps might be telegrams.

"Exactly," said the voice.

"They *are* telegrams?"

"There are no telegrams on Tralfamadore. But you're right: each clump of symbols is a brief, urgent message— describing a situation, a scene. We Tralfamadorians read them all at once, not one after the other. There isn't any particular relationship between all the messages, except that the author has chosen them carefully, so that, when seen all at once, they produce an image of life that is beautiful and surprising and deep. There is no beginning, no middle, no end, no suspense, no moral, no causes, no effects. What we love in our books are the depths of many marvelous moments seen all at one time."

Moments after that, the saucer entered a time warp, and Billy was flung back into his childhood. He was twelve years old, quaking as he stood with his mother and father on Bright Angel Point, at the rim of Grand Canyon. The little human family was staring at the floor of the canyon, one mile straight down.

"Well—" said Billy's father, manfully kicking a pebble into space, "there it *is*." They had come to this famous place by automobile. They had had seven blowouts on the way.

[76]

"It was worth the trip," said Billy's mother raptly. "Oh, God—was it ever *worth* it."

Billy hated the canyon. He was sure that he was going to fall in. His mother touched him, and he wet his pants.

There were other tourists looking down into the canyon, too, and a ranger was there to answer questions. A Frenchman who had come all the way from France asked the ranger in broken English if many people committed suicide by jumping in.

"Yes, sir," said the ranger. "About three folks a year." So it goes.

And Billy took a very short trip through time, made a peewee jump of only ten days, so he was still twelve, still touring the West with his family. Now they were down in Carlsbad Caverns, and Billy was praying to God to get him out of there before the ceiling fell in.

A ranger was explaining that the Caverns had been discovered by a cowboy who saw a huge cloud of bats come out of a hole in the ground. And then he said that he was going to turn out all the lights, and that it would probably be the first time in the lives of most people there that they had ever been in darkness that was total.

Out went the lights. Billy didn't even know whether he was still alive or not. And then something ghostly floated in air to his left. It had numbers on it. His father had taken out his pocket watch. The watch had a radium dial.

Billy went from total dark to total light, found himself back in the war, back in the delousing station again. The shower was over. An unseen hand had turned the water off.

[77]

When Billy got his clothes back, they weren't any cleaner, but all the little animals that had been living in them were dead. So it goes. And his new overcoat was thawed out and limp now. It was much too small for Billy. It had a fur collar and a lining of crimson silk, and had apparently been made for an impresario about as big as an organ-grinder's monkey. It was full of bullet holes.

Billy Pilgrim dressed himself. He put on the little overcoat, too. It split up the back, and, at the shoulders, the sleeves came entirely free. So the coat became a fur-collared vest. It was meant to flare at its owner's waist, but the flaring took place at Billy's armpits. The Germans found him to be one of the most screamingly funny things they had seen in all of World War Two. They laughed and laughed.

And the Germans told everybody else to form in ranks of five, with Billy as their pivot. Then out of doors went the parade, and through gate after gate again. There were more starving Russians with faces like radium dials. The Americans were livelier than before. The jazzing with hot water had cheered them up. And they came to a shed where a corporal with only one arm and one eye wrote the name and serial number of each prisoner in a big, red ledger. Everybody was legally alive now. Before they got their names and numbers in that book, they were missing in action and probably dead.

So it goes.

As the Americans were waiting to move on, an altercation broke out in their rear-most rank. An American had muttered something which a guard did not like. The guard knew English, and he hauled the American out of ranks, knocked him down.

The American was astonished. He stood up shakily, spitting blood. He'd had two teeth knocked out. He had meant no harm by what he'd said, evidently, had no idea that the guard would hear and understand.

"Why me?" he asked the guard.

The guard shoved him back into ranks. "Vy you? Vy anybody?" he said.

When Billy Pilgrim's name was inscribed in the ledger of the prison camp, he was given a number, too, and an iron dogtag in which that number was stamped. A slave laborer from Poland had done the stamping. He was dead now. So it goes.

Billy was told to hang the tag around his neck along with his American dogtags, which he did. The tag was like a salt cracker, perforated down its middle so that a strong man could snap it in two with his bare hands. In case Billy died, which he didn't, half of the tag would mark his body and half would mark his grave.

After poor Edgar Derby, the high school teacher, was shot in Dresden later on, a doctor pronounced him dead and snapped his dogtag in two. So it goes.

Properly enrolled and tagged, the Americans were led through gate after gate again. In two days' time now their families would learn from the International Red Cross that they were alive.

Next to Billy was little Paul Lazzaro, who had promised to avenge Roland Weary. Lazzaro wasn't thinking about vengeance. He was thinking about his terrible bellyache. His stomach had shrunk to the size of a walnut. That dry, shriveled pouch was as sore as a boil.

Next to Lazzaro was poor, doomed old Edgar Derby, with his American and German dogs displayed like a necklace, on the outside of his clothes. He had expected to become a captain, a company commander, because of his wisdom and age. Now here he was on the Czechoslovakian border at midnight.

"Halt," said a guard.

The Americans halted. They stood there quietly in the cold. The sheds they were among were outwardly like thousands of other sheds they had passed. There was this difference, though: the sheds had tin chimneys, and out of the chimneys whirled constellations of sparks.

A guard knocked on a door.

The door was flung open from inside. Light leaped out through the door, escaped from prison at 186,000 miles per second. Out marched fifty middle-aged Englishmen. They were singing "Hail, Hail, the Gang's All Here" from the *Pirates of Penzance*.

These lusty, ruddy vocalists were among the first English-speaking prisoners to be taken in the Second World War. Now they were singing to nearly the last. They had not seen a woman or a child for four years or more. They hadn't seen any birds, either. Not even sparrows would come into the camp.

The Englishmen were officers. Each of them had attempted to escape from another prison at least once. Now they were here, dead-center in a sea of dying Russians.

They could tunnel all they pleased. They would inevitably surface within a rectangle of barbed wire, would find themselves greeted listlessly by dying Russians who spoke no English, who had no food or useful information or escape plans of their own. They could scheme all they pleased to hide aboard a vehicle or steal one, but no vehicle ever came into their compound. They could feign illness, if they liked, but that wouldn't earn them a trip anywhere, either. The only hospital in the camp was a six-bed affair in the British compound itself.

The Englishmen were clean and enthusiastic and decent and strong. They sang boomingly well. They had been singing together every night for years.

The Englishmen had also been lifting weights and chinning themselves for years. Their bellies were like washboards. The muscles of their calves and upper arms were like cannonballs. They were all masters of checkers and chess and bridge and cribbage and dominoes and anagrams and charades and Ping-Pong and billiards, as well.

They were among the wealthiest people in Europe, in terms of food. A clerical error early in the war, when food was still getting through to prisoners, had caused the Red Cross to ship them five hundred parcels every month instead of fifty. The Englishmen had hoarded these so cunningly that now, as the war was ending, they had three tons of sugar, one ton of coffee, eleven hundred pounds of chocolate, seven hundred pounds of tobacco, seventeen hundred pounds of tea, two tons of flour, one ton of canned beef, twelve hundred pounds of canned butter, sixteen hundred pounds of canned cheese, eight hundred pounds of powdered milk, and two tons of orange marmalade.

They kept all this in a room without windows. They had ratproofed it by lining it with flattened tin cans.

They were adored by the Germans, who thought they were exactly what Englishmen ought to be. They made war look stylish and reasonable, and fun. So the Germans let them have four sheds, though one shed would have held them all. And, in exchange for coffee or chocolate or tobacco, the Germans gave them paint and lumber and nails and cloth for fixing things up.

The Englishmen had known for twelve hours that American guests were on their way. They had never had guests before, and they went to work like darling elves, sweeping, mopping, cooking, baking—making mattresses of straw and burlap bags, setting tables, putting party favors at each place.

Now they were singing their welcome to their guests in the winter night. Their clothes were aromatic with the feast they had been preparing. They were dressed half for battle, half for tennis or croquet. They were so elated by their own hospitality, and by all the goodies waiting inside, that they did not take a good look at their guests while they sang. And they imagined that they were singing to fellow officers fresh from the fray.

They wrestled the Americans toward the shed door affectionately, filling the night with manly blather and brotherly rodomontades. They called them "Yank," told them "Good show," promised them that "Jerry was on the run," and so on.

Billy Pilgrim wondered dimly who Jerry was.

Now he was indoors, next to an iron cookstove that was glowing cherry red. Dozens of teapots were boiling there. Some of them had whistles. And there was a witches' cauldron full of golden soup. The soup was thick. Primeval bubbles surfaced it with lethargical majesty as Billy Pilgrim stared.

There were long tables set for a banquet. At each place was a bowl made from a can that had once contained powdered milk. A smaller can was a cup. A taller, more slender can was a tumbler. Each tumbler was filled with warm milk.

At each place was a safety razor, a washcloth, a package of razor blades, a chocolate bar, two cigars, a bar of soap, ten cigarettes, a book of matches, a pencil, and a candle.

Only the candles and the soap were of German origin. They had a ghostly, opalescent similarity. The British had no way of knowing it, but the candles and the soap were made from the fat of rendered Jews and Gypsies and fairies and communists, and other enemies of the State.

So it goes.

The banquet hall was illuminated by candlelight. There were heaps of fresh-baked white bread on the tables, gobs of butter, pots of marmalade. There were platters of sliced beef from cans. Soup and scrambled eggs and hot marmalade pie were yet to come.

And, at the far end of the shed, Billy saw pink arches with azure draperies hanging between them, and an enormous clock, and two golden thrones, and a bucket and a mop. It was in this setting that the evening's entertainment would take place, a musical version of *Cinderella*, the most popular story ever told.

Billy Pilgrim was on fire, having stood too close to the glowing stove. The hem of his little coat was burning. It was a quiet, patient sort of fire—like the burning of punk.

Billy wondered if there was a telephone somewhere. He wanted to call his mother, to tell her he was alive and well.

There was silence now, as the Englishmen looked in astonishment at the frowsy creatures they had so lustily waltzed inside. One of the Englishmen saw that Billy was on fire. "You're on fire, lad!" he said, and he got Billy away from the stove and beat out the sparks with his hands.

When Billy made no comment on this, the Englishman asked him, "Can you talk? Can you hear?"

Billy nodded.

The Englishman touched him exploratorily here and there, filled with pity. "My God—what have they done to you, lad? This isn't a man. It's a broken kite."

"Are you really an American?" said the Englishman.

"Yes," said Billy.

"And your rank?"

"Private."

"What became of your boots, lad?"

"I don't remember."

"Is that coat a *joke?*"

"Sir?"

"Where did you get such a thing?"

Billy had to think hard about that. "They gave it to me," he said at last.

"Jerry gave it to you?"

"Who?"

"The Germans gave it to you?"

"Yes."

Billy didn't like the questions. They were fatiguing.

"Ohhhh—Yank, Yank, Yank—" said the Englishman, "that coat was an *insult.*"

"Sir?"

"It was a deliberate attempt to humiliate you. You mustn't let Jerry do things like that."

Billy Pilgrim swooned.

Billy came to on a chair facing the stage. He had somehow eaten, and now he was watching *Cinderella*. Some part of him had evidently been enjoying the performance for quite a while. Billy was laughing hard.

The women in the play were really men, of course. The clock had just struck midnight, and Cinderella was lamenting:

> "Goodness me, the clock has struck—
> Alackday, and fuck my luck."

Billy found the couplet so comical that he not only laughed—he shrieked. He went on shrieking until he was carried out of the shed and into another, where the hospital was. It was a six-bed hospital. There weren't any other patients in there.

Billy was put to bed and tied down, and given a shot of morphine. Another American volunteered to watch over him. This volunteer was Edgar Derby, the high school teacher who would be shot to death in Dresden. So it goes.

Derby sat on a three-legged stool. He was given a book to read. The book was *The Red Badge of Courage,* by Stephen Crane. Derby had read it before. Now he read it again while Billy Pilgrim entered a morphine paradise.

Under morphine, Billy had a dream of giraffes in a garden. The giraffes were following gravel paths, were pausing to munch sugar pears from treetops. Billy was a giraffe, too. He ate a pear. It was a hard one. It fought back against his grinding teeth. It snapped in juicy protest.

The giraffes accepted Billy as one of their own, as a harmless creature as preposterously specialized as themselves. Two approached him from opposite sides, leaned against him. They had long, muscular upper lips which they could shape like the bells of bugles. They kissed him with these. They were female giraffes—cream and lemon yellow. They had horns like doorknobs. The knobs were covered with velvet.

Why?

Night came to the garden of the giraffes, and Billy Pilgrim slept without dreaming for a while, and then he traveled in time. He woke up with his head under a blanket in a ward for nonviolent mental patients in a veterans' hospital near Lake Placid, New York. It was springtime in 1948, three years after the end of the war.

Billy uncovered his head. The windows of the ward were open. Birds were twittering outside. "Poo-tee-weet?" one asked him. The sun was high. There were twenty-nine other patients assigned to the ward, but they were all outdoors now, enjoying the day. They were free to come and go as they pleased, to go home, even, if they liked—and so was Billy Pilgrim. They had come here voluntarily, alarmed by the outside world.

Billy had committed himself in the middle of his final year at the Ilium School of Optometry. Nobody else suspected that he was going crazy. Everybody else thought he looked fine and was acting fine. Now he was in the hospital. The doctors agreed: He *was* going crazy.

They didn't think it had anything to do with the war. They were sure Billy was going to pieces because his father had thrown him into the deep end of the Y.M.C.A. swimming pool when he was a little boy, and had then taken him to the rim of the Grand Canyon.

The man assigned to the bed next to Billy's was a former infantry captain named Eliot Rosewater. Rosewater was sick and tired of being drunk all the time.

It was Rosewater who introduced Billy to science fiction, and in particular to the writings of Kilgore Trout. Rosewater had a tremendous collection of science-fiction paperbacks under his bed. He had brought them to the hospital in a steamer trunk. Those beloved, frumpish books gave off a smell that permeated the ward—like flannel pajamas that hadn't been changed for a month, or like Irish stew.

Kilgore Trout became Billy's favorite living author, and science fiction became the only sort of tales he could read.

Rosewater was twice as smart as Billy, but he and Billy were dealing with similar crises in similar ways. They had both found life meaningless, partly because of what they had seen in war. Rosewater, for instance, had shot a fourteen-year-old fireman, mistaking him for a German soldier. So it goes. And Billy had seen the greatest massacre in European history, which was the fire-bombing of Dresden. So it goes.

So they were trying to re-invent themselves and their universe. Science fiction was a big help.

Rosewater said an interesting thing to Billy one time about a book that wasn't science fiction. He said that everything there was to know about life was in *The Brothers Karamazov,* by Feodor Dostoevsky. "But that isn't *enough* any more," said Rosewater.

Another time Billy heard Rosewater say to a psychiatrist, "I think you guys are going to have to come up with a lot of wonderful *new* lies, or people just aren't going to want to go on living."

There was a still life on Billy's bedside table—two pills, an ashtray with three lipstick-stained cigarettes in it, one cigarette still burning, and a glass of water. The water was dead. So it goes. Air was trying to get out of that dead water. Bubbles were clinging to the walls of the glass, too weak to climb out.

The cigarettes belonged to Billy's chain-smoking mother. She had sought the ladies' room, which was off the ward for WACS and WAVES and SPARS and WAFS who had gone bananas. She would be back at any moment now.

Billy covered his head with his blanket again. He always covered his head when his mother came to see him in the mental ward—always got much sicker until she went away. It wasn't that she was ugly, or had bad breath or a bad personality. She was a perfectly nice, standard-issue, brown-haired, white woman with a high-school education.

She upset Billy simply by being his mother. She made him feel embarrassed and ungrateful and weak because she had gone to so much trouble to give him life, and to keep that life going, and Billy didn't really like life at all.

Billy heard Eliot Rosewater come in and lie down. Rosewater's bedsprings talked a lot about that. Rosewater was a big man, but not very powerful. He looked as though he might be made out of nose putty.

And then Billy's mother came back from the ladies' room, sat down on a chair between Billy's and Rosewater's bed. Rosewater greeted her with melodious warmth, asked how she was today. He seemed delighted to hear that she was fine. He was experimenting with being ardently sympathetic with everybody he met. He thought that might make the world a slightly more pleasant place to live in. He called Billy's mother "dear." He was experimenting with calling everybody "dear."

"Some day," she promised Rosewater, "I'm going to come in here, and Billy is going to uncover his head, and do you know what he's going to say?"

"What's he going to say, dear?"

"He's going to say, 'Hello, Mom,' and he's going to smile. He's going to say, 'Gee, it's good to see you, Mom. How have you been?' "

"Today could be the day."

"Every night I pray."

"That's a *good* thing to do."

"People would be surprised if they knew how much in this world was due to prayers."

"You never said a truer word, dear."

"Does your mother come to see you often?"

"My mother is dead," said Rosewater. So it goes.

"I'm sorry."

"At least she had a happy life as long as it lasted."

"That's a consolation, anyway."

"Yes."

"Billy's father is dead, you know," said Billy's mother. So it goes.

"A boy *needs* a father."

And on and on it went—that duet between the dumb, praying lady and the big, hollow man who was so full of loving echoes.

"He was at the top of his class when this happened," said Billy's mother.

"Maybe he was *working* too hard," said Rosewater. He

held a book he wanted to read, but he was much too polite to read and talk, too, easy as it was to give Billy's mother satisfactory answers. The book was *Maniacs in the Fourth Dimension,* by Kilgore Trout. It was about people whose mental diseases couldn't be treated because the causes of the diseases were all in the fourth dimension, and three-dimensional Earthling doctors couldn't see those causes at all, or even imagine them.

One thing Trout said that Rosewater liked very much was that there really *were* vampires and werewolves and goblins and angels and so on, but that they were in the fourth dimension. So was William Blake, Rosewater's favorite poet, according to Trout. So were heaven and hell.

"He's engaged to a very rich girl," said Billy's mother.

"That's good," said Rosewater. "Money can be a great comfort sometimes."

"It really *can.*"

"Of course it can."

"It isn't much fun if you have to pinch every penny till it screams."

"It's nice to have a little breathing room."

"Her father owns the optometry school where Billy was going. He also owns six offices around our part of the state. He flies his own plane and has a summer place up on Lake George."

"That's a beautiful lake."

Billy fell asleep under his blanket. When he woke up again, he was tied to the bed in the hospital back in prison. He opened one eye, saw poor old Edgar Derby reading *The Red Badge of Courage* by candlelight. Billy closed that one eye, saw in his memory of the

future poor old Edgar Derby in front of a firing squad in
the ruins of Dresden. There were only four men in that
squad. Billy had heard that one man in each firing squad
was customarily given a rifle loaded with blank cartridge.
Billy didn't think there would be a blank cartridge issued
in a squad that small, in a war that old.

Now the head Englishman came into the hospital to
check on Billy. He was an infantry colonel captured at
Dunkirk. It was he who had given Billy morphine. There
wasn't a real doctor in the compound, so the doctoring was
up to him. "How's the patient?" he asked Derby.

"Dead to the world."

"But not actually dead."

"No."

"How nice—to feel nothing, and still get full credit for
being alive."

Derby now came to lugubrious attention.

"No, no—please—as you were. With only two men for
each officer, and all the men sick, I think we can do
without the usual pageantry between officers and men."

Derby remained standing. "You seem older than the
rest," said the colonel.

Derby told him he was forty-five, which was two years
older than the colonel. The colonel said that the other
Americans had all shaved now, that Billy and Derby were
the only two still with beards. And he said, "You know—
we've had to imagine the war here, and we have imagined
that it was being fought by aging men like ourselves. We
had forgotten that wars were fought by babies. When I saw
those freshly shaved faces, it was a shock. " 'My God, my
God—' I said to myself, 'It's the Children's Crusade.' "

The colonel asked old Derby how he had been captured, and Derby told a tale of being in a clump of trees with about a hundred other frightened soldiers. The battle had been going on for five days. The hundred had been driven into the trees by tanks.

Derby described the incredible artificial weather that Earthlings sometimes create for other Earthlings when they don't want those other Earthlings to inhabit Earth any more. Shells were bursting in the treetops with terrific bangs, he said, showering down knives and needles and razorblades. Little lumps of lead in copper jackets were crisscrossing the woods under the shellbursts, zipping along much faster than sound.

A lot of people were being wounded or killed. So it goes.

Then the shelling stopped, and a hidden German with a loudspeaker told the Americans to put their weapons down and come out of the woods with their hands on the top of their heads, or the shelling would start again. It wouldn't stop until everybody in there was dead.

So the Americans put their weapons down, and they came out of the woods with their hands on top of their heads, because they wanted to go on living, if they possibly could.

Billy traveled in time back to the veterans' hospital again. The blanket was over his head. It was quiet outside the blanket. "Is my mother gone?" said Billy.

"Yes."

Billy peeked out from under his blanket. His fiancée was out there now, sitting on the visitor's chair. Her name was Valencia Merble. Valencia was the daughter of the owner of the Ilium School of Optometry. She was rich. She was as big as a house because she couldn't stop eating. She was eating now. She was eating a Three Musketeers Candy Bar. She was wearing tri-focal lenses in harlequin frames, and the frames were trimmed with rhinestones. The glitter of the rhinestones was answered by the glitter of the diamond in her engagement ring. The diamond was insured for eighteen hundred dollars. Billy had found that diamond in Germany. It was booty of war.

Billy didn't want to marry ugly Valencia. She was one of the symptoms of his disease. He knew he was going crazy when he heard himself proposing marriage to her, when he begged her to take the diamond ring and be his companion for life.

Billy said, "Hello," to her, and she asked him if he wanted some candy, and he said, "No, thanks."

She asked him how he was, and he said, "Much better, thanks." She said that everybody at the Optometry School was sorry he was sick and hoped he would be well soon, and Billy said, "When you see 'em, tell 'em, 'Hello.' "

She promised she would.

She asked him if there was anything she could bring him from the outside, and he said, "No. I have just about everything I want."

"What about books?" said Valencia.

"I'm right next to one of the biggest private libraries in the world," said Billy, meaning Eliot Rosewater's collection of science fiction.

Rosewater was on the next bed, reading, and Billy drew him into the conversation, asked him what he was reading this time.

So Rosewater told him. It was *The Gospel from Outer*

[93]

Space, by Kilgore Trout. It was about a visitor from outer space, shaped very much like a Tralfamadorian, by the way. The visitor from outer space made a serious study of Christianity, to learn, if he could, why Christians found it so easy to be cruel. He concluded that at least part of the trouble was slipshod storytelling in the New Testament. He supposed that the intent of the Gospels was to teach people, among other things, to be merciful, even to the lowest of the low.

But the Gospels actually taught this:

Before you kill somebody, make absolutely sure he isn't well connected. So it goes.

The flaw in the Christ stories, said the visitor from outer space, was that Christ, who didn't look like much, was actually the Son of the Most Powerful Being in the Universe. Readers understood that, so, when they came to the crucifixion, they naturally thought, and Rosewater read out loud again:

Oh, boy—they sure picked the wrong guy to lynch that time!

And that thought had a brother: *"There are* right people *to lynch."* Who? People not well connected. So it goes.

The visitor from outer space made a gift to Earth of a new Gospel. In it, Jesus really *was* a nobody, and a pain in the neck to a lot of people with better connections than he had. He still got to say all the lovely and puzzling things he said in the other Gospels.

So the people amused themselves one day by nailing him to a cross and planting the cross in the ground. There couldn't possibly be any repercussions, the lynchers thought. The reader would have to think that, too, since the new Gospel hammered home again and again what a nobody Jesus was.

And then, just before the nobody died, the heavens opened up, and there was thunder and lightning. The voice of God came crashing down. He told the people that he was adopting the bum as his son, giving him the full powers and privileges of The Son of the Creator of the Universe throughout all eternity. God said this: *From this moment on, He will punish horribly anybody who torments a bum who has no connections!*

Billy's fiancée had finished her Three Musketeers Candy Bar. Now she was eating a Milky Way.

"Forget books," said Rosewater, throwing that particular book under his bed. "The hell with 'em."

"That sounded like an interesting one," said Valencia.

"Jesus—if Kilgore Trout could only *write!*" Rosewater exclaimed. He had a point: Kilgore Trout's unpopularity was deserved. His prose was frightful. Only his ideas were good.

"I don't think Trout has ever been out of the country," Rosewater went on. "My God—he writes about Earthlings all the time, and they're all Americans. Practically nobody on Earth is an American."

"Where does he live?" Valencia asked.

"Nobody knows," Rosewater replied. "I'm the only person who ever heard of him, as far as I can tell. No two books have the same publisher, and every time I write him in care of a publisher, the letter comes back because the publisher has failed."

He changed the subject now, congratulated Valencia on her engagement ring.

"Thank you," she said, and held it out so Rosewater could get a close look. "Billy got that diamond in the war."

"That's the attractive thing about war," said Rosewater. "Absolutely everybody gets a little something."

With regard to the whereabouts of Kilgore Trout: he actually lived in Ilium, Billy's hometown, friendless and despised. Billy would meet him by and by.

"Billy—" said Valencia Merble.

"Hm?"

"You want to talk about our silver pattern?"

"Sure."

"I've got it narrowed down pretty much to either Royal Danish or Rambler Rose."

"Rambler Rose," said Billy.

"It isn't something we should *rush* into," she said. "I mean—whatever we decide on, that's what we're going to have to live with the rest of our lives."

Billy studied the pictures. "Royal Danish," he said at last.

"Colonial Moonlight is nice, too."

"Yes, it is," said Billy Pilgrim.

And Billy traveled in time to the zoo on Tralfamadore. He was forty-four years old, on display under a geodesic dome. He was reclining on the lounge chair which had been his cradle during his trip through space. He was naked. The Tralfamadorians were interested in his body— *all* of it. There were thousands of them outside, holding up their little hands so that their eyes could see him. Billy had been on Tralfamadore for six Earthling months now. He was used to the crowd.

Escape was out of the question. The atmosphere outside the dome was cyanide, and Earth was 446,120,000,000,000,000 miles away.

Billy was displayed there in the zoo in a simulated Earthling habitat. Most of the furnishings had been stolen from the Sears & Roebuck warehouse in Iowa City, Iowa. There was a color television set and a couch that could be converted into a bed. There were end tables with lamps and ashtrays on them by the couch. There was a home bar and two stools. There was a little pool table. There was wall-to-wall carpeting in federal gold, except in the kitchen and bathroom areas and over the iron manhole cover in the center of the floor. There were magazines arranged in a fan on the coffee table in front of the couch.

There was a stereophonic phonograph. The phonograph worked. The television didn't. There was a picture of one cowboy killing another one pasted to the television tube. So it goes.

There were no walls in the dome, no place for Billy to hide. The mint green bathroom fixtures were right out in the open. Billy got off his lounge chair now, went into the bathroom and took a leak. The crowd went wild.

Billy brushed his teeth on Tralfamadore, put in his partial denture, and went into his kitchen. His bottled-gas range and his refrigerator and his dishwasher were mint green, too. There was a picture painted on the door of the refrigerator. The refrigerator had come that way. It was a picture of a Gay Nineties couple on a bicycle built for two.

Billy looked at that picture now, tried to think some·
thing about the couple. Nothing came to him. There
didn't seem to be *anything* to think about those two
people.

Billy ate a good breakfast from cans. He washed his cup
and plate and knife and fork and spoon and saucepan, put
them away. Then he did exercises he had learned in the
Army—straddle jumps, deep knee bends, sit-ups and push-
ups. Most Tralfamadorians had no way of knowing Billy's
body and face were not beautiful. They supposed that he
was a splendid specimen. This had a pleasant effect on
Billy, who began to enjoy his body for the first time.

He showered after his exercises and trimmed his toe-
nails. He shaved, and sprayed deodorant under his arms,
while a zoo guide on a raised platform outside explained
what Billy was doing—and why. The guide was lecturing
telepathically, simply standing there, sending out thought
waves to the crowd. On the platform with him was the
little keyboard instrument with which he would relay
questions to Billy from the crowd.

Now the first question came—from the speaker on the
television set: "Are you happy here?"

"About as happy as I was on Earth," said Billy Pilgrim,
which was true.

There were five sexes on Tralfamadore, each of them
performing a step necessary in the creation of a new
individual. They looked identical to Billy—because their
sex differences were all in the fourth dimension.

One of the biggest moral bombshells handed to Billy by
the Tralfamadorians, incidentally, had to do with sex on
Earth. They said their flying-saucer crews had identified no

[98]

fewer than *seven* sexes on Earth, each essential to reproduction. Again: Billy couldn't possibly imagine what five of those seven sexes had to do with the making of a baby, since they were sexually active only in the fourth dimension.

The Tralfamadorians tried to give Billy clues that would help him imagine sex in the invisible dimension. They told him that there could be no Earthling babies without male homosexuals. There *could* be babies without female homosexuals. There couldn't be babies without women over sixty-five years old. There *could* be babies without men over sixty-five. There couldn't be babies without other babies who had lived an hour or less after birth. And so on.

It was gibberish to Billy.

There was a lot that Billy said that was gibberish to the Tralfamadorians, too. They couldn't imagine what time looked like to him. Billy had given up on explaining that. The guide outside had to explain as best he could.

The guide invited the crowd to imagine that they were looking across a desert at a mountain range on a day that was twinkling bright and clear. They could look at a peak or a bird or a cloud, at a stone right in front of them, or even down into a canyon behind them. But among them was this poor Earthling, and his head was encased in a steel sphere which he could never take off. There was only one eyehole through which he could look, and welded to that eyehole were six feet of pipe.

This was only the beginning of Billy's miseries in the metaphor. He was also strapped to a steel lattice which was bolted to a flatcar on rails, and there was no way he could turn his head or touch the pipe. The far end of the pipe rested on a bi-pod which was also bolted to the flatcar. All Billy could see was the little dot at the end of the pipe. He didn't know he was on a flatcar, didn't even know there was anything peculiar about his situation.

The flatcar sometimes crept, sometimes went extremely fast, often stopped—went uphill, downhill, around curves, along straightaways. Whatever poor Billy saw through the pipe, he had no choice but to say to himself, "That's life."

Billy expected the Tralfamadorians to be baffled and alarmed by all the wars and other forms of murder on Earth. He expected them to fear that the Earthling combination of ferocity and spectacular weaponry might eventually destroy part or maybe all of the innocent Universe. Science fiction had led him to expect that.

But the subject of war never came up until Billy brought it up himself. Somebody in the zoo crowd asked him through the lecturer what the most valuable thing he had learned on Tralfamadore was so far, and Billy replied, "How the inhabitants of a whole planet can live in peace! As you know, I am from a planet that has been engaged in senseless slaughter since the beginning of time. I myself have seen the bodies of schoolgirls who were boiled alive in a water tower by my own countrymen, who were proud of fighting pure evil at the time." This was true. Billy saw the boiled bodies in Dresden. "And I have lit my way in a prison at night with candles from the fat of human beings who were butchered by the brothers and fathers of those schoolgirls who were boiled. Earthlings must be the terrors of the Universe! If other planets aren't now in danger from Earth, they soon will be. So tell me the secret so I can take it back to Earth and save us all: How can a planet live at peace?"

Billy felt that he had spoken soaringly. He was baffled when he saw the Tralfamadorians close their little hands on their eyes. He knew from past experience what this meant: He was being stupid.

"Would—would you mind telling me—" he said to the guide, much deflated, "what was so stupid about that?"

"We know how the Universe ends—" said the guide, "and Earth has nothing to do with it, except that *it* gets wiped out, too."

"How—how *does* the Universe end?" said Billy.

"We blow it up, experimenting with new fuels for our flying saucers. A Tralfamadorian test pilot presses a starter button, and the whole Universe disappears." So it goes.

"If you know this," said Billy, "isn't there some way you can prevent it? Can't you keep the pilot from *pressing* the button?"

"He has *always* pressed it, and he always *will*. We *always* let him and we always *will* let him. The moment is *structured* that way."

"So—" said Billy gropingly, "I suppose that the idea of preventing war on Earth is stupid, too."

"Of course."

"But you *do* have a peaceful planet here."

"Today we do. On other days we have wars as horrible as any you've ever seen or read about. There isn't anything we can do about them, so we simply don't look at them. We ignore them. We spend eternity looking at pleasant moments—like today at the zoo. Isn't this a nice moment?"

"Yes."

"That's one thing Earthlings might learn to do, if they

tried hard enough: Ignore the awful times, and concentrate on the good ones."

"Um," said Billy Pilgrim.

Shortly after he went to sleep that night, Billy traveled in time to another moment which was quite nice, his wedding night with the former Valencia Merble. He had been out of the veterans' hospital for six months. He was all well. He had graduated from the Ilium School of Optometry—third in his class of forty-seven.

Now he was in bed with Valencia in a delightful studio apartment which was built on the end of a wharf on Cape Ann, Massachusetts. Across the water were the lights of Gloucester. Billy was on top of Valencia, making love to her. One result of this act would be the birth of Robert Pilgrim, who would become a problem in high school, but who would then straighten out as a member of the famous Green Berets.

Valencia wasn't a time-traveler, but she did have a lively imagination. While Billy was making love to her, she imagined that she was a famous woman in history. She was being Queen Elizabeth the First of England, and Billy was supposedly Christopher Columbus.

Billy made a noise like a small, rusty hinge. He had just emptied his seminal vesicles into Valencia, had contributed his share of the Green Beret. According to the Tralfamadorians, of course, the Green Beret would have seven parents in all.

Now he rolled off his huge wife, whose rapt expression did not change when he departed. He lay with the buttons of his spine along the edge of the mattress, folded his hands behind his head. He was rich now. He had been rewarded for marrying a girl nobody in his right mind would have married. His father-in-law had given him a new Buick Roadmaster, an all-electric home, and had made him manager of his most prosperous office, his Ilium office, where Billy could expect to make at least thirty thousand dollars a year. That was good. His father had been only a barber.

As his mother said, "The Pilgrims are coming up in the world."

The honeymoon was taking place in the bittersweet mysteries of Indian Summer in New England. The lovers' apartment had one romantic wall which was all Franch doors. They opened onto a balcony and the oily harbor beyond.

A green and orange dragger, black in the night, grumbled and drummed past their balcony, not thirty feet from their wedding bed. It was going to sea with only its running lights on. Its empty holds were resonant, made the song of the engines rich and loud. The wharf began to sing the same song, and then the honeymooners' headboard sang, too. And it continued to sing long after the dragger was gone.

"Thank you," said Valencia at last. The headboard was singing a mosquito song.

"You're welcome."

"It was nice."

"I'm glad."

Then she began to cry.

"What's the matter?"

"I'm so happy."

"Good."

"I never thought anybody would marry me."

"Um," said Billy Pilgrim.

"I'm going to lose weight for you," she said.

"What?"

"I'm going to go on a diet. I'm going to become beautiful for you."

"I like you just the way you are."

"Do you *really?*"

"Really," said Billy Pilgrim. He had already seen a lot of their marriage, thanks to time-travel, knew that it was going to be at least bearable all the way.

A great motor yacht named the *Scheherezade* now slid past the marriage bed. The song its engines sang was a very low organ note. All her lights were on.

Two beautiful people, a young man and a young woman in evening clothes, were at the rail in the stern, loving each other and their dreams and the wake. They were honeymooning, too. They were Lance Rumfoord, of Newport, Rhode Island, and his bride, the former Cynthia Landry, who had been a childhood sweetheart of John F. Kennedy in Hyannis Port, Massachusetts.

There was a slight coincidence here. Billy Pilgrim would later share a hospital room with Rumfoord's uncle, Professor Bertram Copeland Rumfoord of Harvard, official Historian of the United States Air Force.

When the beautiful people were past, Valencia questioned her funny-looking husband about war. It was a simple-minded thing for a female Earthling to do, to associate sex and glamor with war.

"Do you ever think about the war?" she said, laying a hand on his thigh.

"Sometimes," said Billy Pilgrim.

"I look at you sometimes," said Valencia, "and I get a funny feeling that you're just full of secrets."

"I'm not," said Billy. This was a lie, of course. He hadn't told anybody about all the time-traveling he'd done, about Tralfamadore and so on.

"You must have secrets about the war. Or, not secrets, I guess, but things you don't want to talk about."

"No."

"I'm *proud* you were a soldier. Do you know that?"

"Good."

"Was it awful?"

"Sometimes." A crazy thought now occurred to Billy. The truth of it startled him. It would make a good epitaph for Billy Pilgrim—and for me, too.

"Would you talk about the war now, if I *wanted* you to?" said Valencia. In a tiny cavity in her great body she was assembling the materials for a Green Beret.

"It would sound like a dream," said Billy. "Other people's dreams aren't very interesting, usually."

"I heard you tell Father one time about a German firing squad." She was referring to the execution of poor old Edgar Derby.

"Um."

"You had to bury him?"

"Yes."

"Did he see you with your shovels before he was shot?"

"Yes."

"Did he *say* anything?"

"No."

"Was he *scared*?"

"They had him doped up. He was sort of glassy-eyed."

"And they pinned a target to him?"

"A piece of paper," said Billy. He got out of bed, said, "Excuse me," went into the darkness of the bathroom to

EVERYTHING
WAS
BEAUTIFUL,
AND
NOTHING
HURT

take a leak. He groped for the light, realized as he felt the rough walls that he had traveled back to 1944, to the prison hospital again.

The candle in the hospital had gone out. Poor old Edgar Derby had fallen asleep on the cot next to Billy's. Billy was out of bed, groping along a wall, trying to find a way out because he had to take a leak so badly.

He suddenly found a door, which opened, let him reel out into the prison night. Billy was loony with time-travel and morphine. He delivered himself to a barbed-wire fence which snagged him in a dozen places. Billy tried to back away from it, but the barbs wouldn't let go. So Billy did a silly little dance with the fence, taking a step this way, then that way, then returning to the beginning again.

A Russian, himself out in the night to take a leak, saw Billy dancing—from the other side of the fence. He came over to the curious scarecrow, tried to talk with it gently, asked it what country it was from. The scarecrow paid no attention, went on dancing. So the Russian undid the snags one by one, and the scarecrow danced off into the night again without a word of thanks.

The Russian waved to him, and called after him in Russian, "Good-bye."

Billy took his pecker out, there in the prison night, and peed and peed on the ground. Then he put it away again, more or less, and contemplated a new problem: Where had he come from, and where should he go now?

Somewhere in the night there were cries of grief. With nothing better to do, Billy shuffled in their direction. He wondered what tragedy so many had found to lament out of doors.

Billy was approaching, without knowing it, the back of the latrine. It consisted of a one-rail fence with twelve buckets underneath it. The fence was sheltered on three sides by a screen of scrap lumber and flattened tin cans. The open side faced the black tarpaper wall of the shed where the feast had taken place.

Billy moved along the screen and reached a point where he could see a message freshly painted on the tarpaper wall. The words were written with the same pink paint which had brightened the set for *Cinderella*. Billy's perceptions were so unreliable that he saw the words as hanging in air, painted on a transparent curtain, perhaps. And there were lovely silver dots on the curtain, too. These were really nailheads holding the tarpaper to the shed. Billy could not imagine how the curtain was supported in nothingness, and he supposed that the magic curtain and the theatrical grief were part of some religious ceremony he knew nothing about.

Here is what the message said:

PLEASE LEAVE THIS LATRINE AS TIDY AS YOU FOUND IT!

Billy looked inside the latrine. The wailing was coming from in there. The place was crammed with Americans who had taken their pants down. The welcome feast had made them as sick as volcanoes. The buckets were full or had been kicked over.

An American near Billy wailed that he had excreted everything but his brains. Moments later he said, "There they go, there they go." He meant his brains.

That was I. That was me. That was the author of this book.

Billy reeled away from his vision of Hell. He passed three Englishmen who were watching the excrement festival from a distance. They were catatonic with disgust.

"Button your pants!" said one as Billy went by.

So Billy buttoned his pants. He came to the door of the little hospital by accident. He went through the door, and found himself honeymooning again, going from the bathroom back to bed with his bride on Cape Ann.

"I missed you," said Valencia.

"I missed *you*," said Billy Pilgrim.

Billy and Valencia went to sleep nestled like spoons, and Billy traveled in time back to the train ride he had taken in 1944—from maneuvers in South Carolina to his father's funeral in Ilium. He hadn't seen Europe or combat yet. This was still in the days of steam locomotives.

Billy had to change trains a lot. All the trains were slow. The coaches stunk of coal smoke and rationed tobacco and rationed booze and the farts of people eating wartime food. The upholstery of the iron seats was bristly, and Billy couldn't sleep much. He got to sleep soundly when he was only three hours from Ilium, with his legs splayed toward the entrance of the busy dining car.

The porter woke him up when the train reached Ilium. Billy staggered off with his duffel bag, and then he stood on the station platform next to the porter, trying to wake up.

"Have a good nap, did you?" said the porter.

"Yes," said Billy.

"Man," said the porter, "you sure had a hard-on."

At three in the morning on Billy's morphine night in prison, a new patient was carried into the hospital by two lusty Englishmen. He was tiny. He was Paul Lazzaro, the polka-dotted car thief from Cicero, Illinois. He had been caught stealing cigarettes from under the pillow of an Englishman. The Englishman, half asleep, had broken Lazzaro's right arm and knocked him unconscious.

The Englishman who had done this was helping to carry Lazzaro in now. He had fiery red hair and no eyebrows. He had been Cinderella's Blue Fairy Godmother in the play. Now he supported his half of Lazzaro with one hand while he closed the door behind himself with the other. "Doesn't weigh as much as a chicken," he said.

The Englishman with Lazzaro's feet was the colonel who had given Billy his knock-out shot.

The Blue Fairy Godmother was embarrassed, and angry, too. "If I'd known I was fighting a chicken," he said, "I wouldn't have fought so *hard*."

"Um."

The Blue Fairy Godmother spoke frankly about how disgusting all the Americans were. "Weak, smelly, self-pitying—a pack of sniveling, dirty, thieving bastards," he said. "They're worse than the bleeding Russians."

"*Do* seem a scruffy lot," the colonel agreed.

A German major came in now. He considered the Englishmen as close friends. He visited them nearly every day, played games with them, lectured to them on German history, played their piano, gave them lessons in conversational German. He told them often that, if it weren't for their civilized company, he would go mad. His English was splendid.

He was apologetic about the Englishmen's having to put up with the American enlisted men. He promised them that they would not be inconvenienced for more than a day or two, that the Americans would soon be shipped to Dresden as contract labor. He had a monograph with him, published by the German Association of Prison Officials. It was a report on the behavior in Germany of American enlisted men as prisoners of war. It was written by a former American who had risen high in the German Ministry of Propaganda. His name was Howard W. Campbell, Jr. He would later hang himself while awaiting trial as a war criminal.

So it goes.

While the British colonel set Lazzaro's broken arm and mixed plaster for the cast, the German major translated out loud passages from Howard W. Campbell, Jr.'s monograph. Campbell had been a fairly well-known playwright at one time. His opening line was this one:

America is the wealthiest nation on Earth, but its people are mainly poor, and poor Americans are urged to hate themselves. To quote the American humorist Kin Hubbard, "It ain't no disgrace to be poor, but it might as well be." It is in fact a crime for an American to be poor, even though America is a nation of poor. Every other nation has folk traditions of men who were poor but extremely wise and virtuous, and therefore more estimable than anyone with power and gold. No such tales are told by the American poor. They mock themselves and glorify their betters. The meanest eating or drinking establishment, owned by a man who is himself poor, is very likely to have a sign on its wall asking this cruel question: "If you're so smart, why ain't you rich?" There will also be an American flag no larger than a child's hand—glued to a lollipop stick and flying from the cash register.

The author of the monograph, a native of Schenectady, New York, was said by some to have had the highest I.Q. of all the war criminals who were made to face a death by hanging. So it goes.

Americans, like human beings everywhere, believe many things that are obviously untrue, the monograph went on. *Their most destructive untruth is that it is very easy for any American to make money. They will not acknowledge how in fact hard money is to come by, and, therefore, those who have no money blame and blame and blame themselves. This inward blame has been a treasure for the rich and powerful, who have had to do less for their poor, publicly and privately, than any other ruling class since, say, Napoleonic times.*

Many novelties have come from America. The most startling of these, a thing without precedent, is a mass of undignified poor. They do not love one another because they do not love themselves. Once this is understood, the disagreeable behavior of American enlisted men in German prisons ceases to be a mystery.

Howard W. Campbell, Jr., now discussed the uniform of the American enlisted in World War Two: *Every other army in history, prosperous or not, has attempted to clothe even its lowliest soldiers so as to make them impressive to themselves and others as stylish experts in drinking and copulation and looting and sudden death. The American*

Army, however, sends its enlisted men out to fight and die in a modified business suit quite evidently made for another man, a sterilized but unpressed gift from a nose-holding charity which passes out clothing to drunks in the slums.

When a dashingly-clad officer addresses such a frumpishly dressed bum, he scolds him, as an officer in any army must. But the officer's contempt is not, as in other armies, avuncular theatricality. It is a genuine expression of hatred for the poor, who have no one to blame for their misery but themselves.

A prison administrator dealing with captured American enlisted men for the first time should be warned: Expect no brotherly love, even between brothers. There will be no cohesion between the individuals. Each will be a sulky child who often wishes he were dead.

Campbell told what the German experience with captured American enlisted men had been. They were known everywhere to be the most self-pitying, least fraternal, and dirtiest of all prisoners of war, said Campbell. They were incapable of concerted action on their own behalf. They despised any leader from among their own number, refused to follow or even listen to him, on the grounds that he was no better than they were, that he should stop putting on airs.

And so on. Billy Pilgrim went to sleep, woke up as a widower in his empty home in Ilium. His daughter Barbara was reproaching him for writing ridiculous letters to the newspapers.

"Did you hear what I said?" Barbara inquired. It was 1968 again.

[113]

"Of course." He had been dozing.

"If you're going to act like a child, maybe we'll just have to *treat* you like a child."

"That isn't what happens next," said Billy.

"We'll *see* what happens next." Big Barbara now embraced herself. "It's awfully cold in here. Is the heat on?"

"The *heat?*"

"The furnace—the thing in the basement, the thing that makes hot air that comes out of these registers. I don't think it's working."

"Maybe not."

"Aren't you cold?"

"I hadn't noticed."

"Oh my God, you *are* a child. If we leave you alone here, you'll freeze to death, you'll starve to death." And so on. It was very exciting for her, taking his dignity away in the name of love.

Barbara called the oil-burner man, and she made Billy go to bed, made him promise to stay under the electric blanket until the heat came on. She set the control of the blanket at the highest notch, which soon made Billy's bed hot enough to bake bread in.

When Barbara left, slamming the door behind her, Billy traveled in time to the zoo on Tralfamadore again. A mate had just been brought to him from Earth. She was Montana Wildhack, a motion picture star.

Montana was under heavy sedation. Tralfamadorians wearing gas masks brought her in, put her on Billy's yellow lounge chair; withdrew through his airlock. The vast crowd outside was delighted. All attendance records for the zoo were broken. Everybody on the planet wanted to see the Earthlings mate.

Montana was naked, and so was Billy, of course. He had a tremendous wang, incidentally. You never know who'll get one.

Now she fluttered her eyelids. Her lashes were like buggy whips. "Where *am* I?" she said.

"Everything is all right," said Billy gently. "Please don't be afraid."

Montana had been unconscious during her trip from Earth. The Tralfamadorians hadn't talked to her, hadn't shown themselves to her. The last thing she remembered was sunning herself by a swimming pool in Palm Springs, California. Montana was only twenty years old. Around her neck was a silver chain with a heart-shaped locket hanging from it—between her breasts.

Now she turned her head to see the myriads of Tralfamadorians outside the dome. They were applauding her by opening and closing their little green hands quickly.

Montana screamed and screamed.

All the little green hands closed tight, because Montana's terror was so unpleasant to see. The head zoo keeper ordered a crane operator, who was standing by, to drop a navy blue canopy over the dome, thus simulating Earthling night inside. Real night came to the zoo for only one Earthling hour out of every sixty-two.

Billy switched on a floor lamp. The light from the single source threw the baroque detailing of Montana's body into sharp relief. Billy was reminded of fantastic architecture in Dresden, before it was bombed.

In time, Montana came to love and trust Billy Pilgrim. He did not touch her until she made it clear that she wanted him to. After she had been on Tralfamadore for what would have been an Earthling week, she asked him shyly if he wouldn't sleep with her. Which he did. It was heavenly.

And Billy traveled in time from that delightful bed to a bed in 1968. It was his bed in Ilium, and the electric blanket was turned up high. He was drenched in sweat, remembered groggily that his daughter had put him to bed, had told him to stay there until the oil burner was repaired.

Somebody was knocking on his bedroom door.

"Yes?" said Billy.

"Oil-burner man."

"Yes?"

"It's running good now. Heat's coming up."

"Good."

"Mouse ate through a wire from the thermostat."

"I'll be darned."

Billy sniffed. His hot bed smelled like a mushroom cellar. He had had a wet dream about Montana Wildhack.

On the morning after that wet dream, Billy decided to go back to work in his office in the shopping plaza. Business was booming as usual. His assistants were keeping up with it nicely. They were startled to see him. They had been told by his daughter that he might never practice again.

But Billy went into his examining room briskly, asked that the first patient be sent in. So they sent him one—a twelve-year-old boy who was accompanied by his widowed mother. They were strangers, new in town. Billy asked them a little about themselves, learned that the boy's father had been killed in Vietnam—in the famous five-day battle for Hill 875 near Dakto. So it goes.

While he examined the boy's eyes, Billy told him matter-of-factly about his adventures on Tralfamadore, assured the fatherless boy that his father was very much alive still in moments the boy would see again and again.

"Isn't that comforting?" Billy asked.

And somewhere in there, the boy's mother went out and told the receptionist that Billy was evidently going crazy. Billy was taken home. His daughter asked him again, "Father, Father, Father—what *are* we going to *do* with you?"

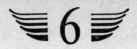

6

Listen:

Billy Pilgrim says he went to Dresden, Germany, on the day after his morphine night in the British compound in the center of the extermination camp for Russian prisoners of war. Billy woke up at dawn on that day in January. There were no windows in the little hospital, and the ghostly candles had gone out. So the only light came from pin-prick holes in the walls, and from a sketchy rectangle that outlined the imperfectly fitted door. Little Paul Lazzaro, with a broken arm, snored on one bed. Edgar Derby, the high school teacher who would eventually be shot, snored on another.

Billy sat up in bed. He had no idea what year it was or what planet he was on. Whatever the planet's name was, it was cold. But it wasn't the cold that had awakened Billy. It was animal magnetism which was making him shiver and itch. It gave him profound aches in his musculature, as though he had been exercising hard.

The animal magnetism was coming from behind him. If Billy had had to guess as to the source, he would have said that there was a vampire bat hanging upside down on the wall behind him.

Billy moved down toward the foot of his cot before turning to look at whatever it was. He didn't want the animal to drop into his face and maybe claw his eyes out or bite off his big nose. Then he turned. The source of the magnetism really did resemble a bat. It was Billy's impresario's coat with the fur collar. It was hanging from a nail.

Billy now backed toward it again, looking at it over his shoulder, feeling the magnetism increase. Then he faced it, kneeling on his cot, dared to touch it here and there. He was seeking the exact source of the radiations.

He found two small sources, two lumps an inch apart and hidden in the lining. One was shaped like a pea. The other was shaped like a tiny horseshoe. Billy received a message carried by the radiations. He was told not to find out what the lumps were. He was advised to be content with knowing that they could work miracles for him, provided he did not insist on learning their nature. That was all right with Billy Pilgrim. He was grateful. He was glad.

Billy dozed, awakened in the prison hospital again. The sun was high. Outside were Golgotha sounds of strong men digging holes for upright timbers in hard, hard ground. Englishmen were building themselves a new latrine. They had abandoned their old latrine to the Americans—and their theater, the place where the feast had been held, too.

Six Englishmen staggered through a hospital with a pool table on which several mattresses were piled. They were transferring it to living quarters attached to the hospital. They were followed by an Englishman dragging his mattress and carrying a dartboard.

The man with the dartboard was the Blue Fairy Godmother who had injured little Paul Lazzaro. He stopped by Lazzaro's bed, asked Lazzaro how he was.

Lazzaro told him he was going to have him killed after the war.

"Oh?"

"You made a big mistake," said Lazzaro. "Anybody touches me, he better *kill* me, or I'm gonna have *him* killed."

The Blue Fairy Godmother knew something about killing. He gave Lazzaro a careful smile. "There is still time for *me* to kill *you*," he said, "if you really persuade me that it's the sensible thing to do."

"Why don't you go fuck yourself?"

"Don't think I haven't tried," the Blue Fairy Godmother answered.

The Blue Fairy Godmother left, amused and patronizing. When he was gone, Lazzaro promised Billy and poor old Edgar Derby that he was going to have revenge, and that revenge was sweet.

"It's the sweetest thing there is," said Lazzaro. "People fuck with me," he said, "and Jesus Christ are they ever fucking sorry. I laugh like hell. I don't care if it's a guy or a dame. If the President of the United States fucked around with me, I'd fix him good. You should have seen what I did to a dog one time."

"A dog?" said Billy.

"Son of a bitch bit me. So I got me some steak, and I got me the spring out of a clock. I cut that spring up in little pieces. I put points on the ends of the pieces. They were sharp as razor blades. I stuck 'em into the steak—way inside. And I went past where they had the dog tied up. He wanted to bite me again. I said to him, 'Come on, doggie—let's be friends. Let's not be enemies any more. I'm not mad.' He believed me."

"He *did?*"

"I threw him the steak. He swallowed it down in one big gulp. I waited around for ten minutes." Now Lazzaro's eyes twinkled. "Blood started coming out of his mouth. He started crying, and he rolled on the ground, as though the knives were on the outside of him instead of on the inside of him. Then he tried to bite out his own insides. I laughed, and I said to him, 'You got the right idea now. Tear your own guts out, boy. That's *me* in there with all those knives.'" So it goes.

"Anybody ever asks you what the sweetest thing in life is—" said Lazzaro, "it's revenge."

When Dresden was destroyed later on, incidentally, Lazzaro did not exult. He didn't have anything against the Germans, he said. Also, he said he liked to take his enemies one at a time. He was proud of never having hurt an innocent bystander. "Nobody ever got it from Lazzaro," he said, "who didn't have it coming."

Poor old Edgar Derby, the high school teacher, got into the conversation now. He asked Lazzaro if he planned to feed the Blue Fairy Godmother clock springs and steak.

"Shit," said Lazzaro.

"He's a pretty big man," said Derby, who, of course, was a pretty big man himself.

"Size don't mean a thing."

"You're going to *shoot* him?"

"I'm gonna *have* him shot," said Lazzaro. "He'll get home after the war. He'll be a big hero. The dames'll be climbing all over him. He'll settle down. A couple of years'll go by. And then one day there'll be a knock on his door. He'll answer the door, and there'll be a stranger out there. The stranger'll ask him if he's so-and-so. When he says he is, the stranger'll say, 'Paul Lazzaro sent me.' And he'll pull out a gun and shoot his pecker off. The stranger'll let him think a couple of seconds about who Paul Lazzaro is and what life's gonna be like without a pecker. Then he'll shoot him once in the guts and walk away." So it goes.

Lazzaro said that he could have anybody in the world killed for a thousand dollars plus traveling expenses. He had a list in his head, he said.

Derby asked him who all was on the list, and Lazzaro said, "Just make fucking sure *you* don't get on it. Just don't cross me, that's all." There was a silence, and then he added, "And don't cross my friends."

"You have *friends?*" Derby wanted to know.

"In the *war?*" said Lazzaro. "Yeah—I had a friend in the war. He's dead." So it goes.

"That's too bad."

Lazzaro's eyes were twinkling again. "Yeah. He was my buddy on the boxcar. His name was Roland Weary. He died in my arms." Now he pointed to Billy with his one mobile hand. "He died on account of this silly cocksucker here. So I promised him I'd have this silly cocksucker shot after the war."

Lazzaro erased with his hand anything Billy Pilgrim might be about to say. "Just forget about it, kid," he said. "Enjoy life while you can. Nothing's gonna happen for maybe five, ten, fifteen, twenty years. But lemme give you a piece of advice: Whenever the doorbell rings, have somebody else answer the door."

Billy Pilgrim says now that this really is the way he *is* going to die, too. As a time-traveler, he has seen his own death many times, has described it to a tape recorder. The tape is locked up with his will and some other valuables in his safe-deposit box at the Ilium Merchants National Bank and Trust, he says.

I, Billy Pilgrim, the tape begins, *will die, have died, and always will die on February thirteenth, 1976.*

At the time of his death, he says, he is in Chicago to address a large crowd on the subject of flying saucers and the true nature of time. His home is still in Ilium. He has had to cross three international boundaries in order to reach Chicago. The United States of America has been Balkanized, has been divided into twenty petty nations so that it will never again be a threat to world peace. Chicago has been hydrogen-bombed by angry Chinamen. So it goes. It is all brand new.

Billy is speaking before a capacity audience in a baseball park, which is covered by a geodesic dome. The flag of the country is behind him. It is a Hereford bull on a field of green. Billy predicts his own death within an hour. He laughs about it, invites the crowd to laugh with him. "It is high time I was dead," he says. "Many years ago," he said, "a certain man promised to have me killed. He is an old man now, living not far from here. He has read all the publicity associated with my appearance in your fair city. He is insane. Tonight he will keep his promise."

There are protests from the crowd.

Billy Pilgrim rebukes them. "If you protest, if you think that death is a terrible thing, then you have not understood a word I've said." Now he closes his speech as he closes every speech—with these words: "Farewell, hello, farewell, hello."

There are police around him as he leaves the stage. They are there to protect him from the crush of popularity. No threats on his life have been made since 1945. The

[123]

police offer to stay with him. They are floridly willing to stand in a circle around him all night, with their zap guns drawn.

"No, no," says Billy serenely. "It is time for you to go home to your wives and children, and it is time for me to be dead for a little while—and then live again." At that moment, Billy's high forehead is in the cross hairs of a high-powered laser gun. It is aimed at him from the darkened press box. In the next moment, Billy Pilgrim is dead. So it goes.

So Billy experiences death for a while. It is simply violet light and a hum. There isn't anybody else there. Not even Billy Pilgrim is there.

Then he swings back into life again, all the way back to an hour after his life was threatened by Lazzaro—in 1945. He has been told to get out of his hospital bed and dress, that he is well. He and Lazzaro and poor old Edgar Derby are to join their fellows in the theater. There they will choose a leader for themselves by secret ballot in a free election.

Billy and Lazzaro and poor old Edgar Derby crossed the prison yard to the theater now. Billy was carrying his little coat as though it were a lady's muff. It was wrapped around and around his hands. He was the central clown in an unconscious travesty of that famous oil painting, "The Spirit of '76."

Edgar Derby was writing letters home in his head, telling his wife that he was alive and well, that she shouldn't worry, that the war was nearly over, that he would soon be home.

Lazzaro was talking to himself about people he was

going to have killed after the war, and rackets he was going to work, and women he was going to make fuck him, whether they wanted to or not. If he had been a dog in a city, a policeman would have shot him and sent his head to a laboratory, to see if he had rabies. So it goes.

As they neared the theater, they came upon an Englishman who was hacking a groove in the Earth with the heel of his boot. He was marking the boundary between the American and English sections of the compound. Billy and Lazzaro and Derby didn't have to ask what the line meant. It was a familiar symbol from childhood.

The theater was paved with American bodies that nestled like spoons. Most of the Americans were in stupors or asleep. Their guts were fluttering, dry.

"Close the fucking door," somebody said to Billy. "Were you born in a barn?"

Billy closed it, took a hand from his muff, touched a stove. It was as cold as ice. The stage was still set for *Cinderella*. Azure curtains hung from arches which were shocking pink. There were golden thrones and the dummy clock, whose hands were set at midnight. Cinderella's slippers, which were airman's boots painted silver, were capsized side by side under a golden throne.

Billy and poor old Edgar Derby and Lazzaro had been in the hospital when the British passed out blankets and mattresses, so they had none. They had to improvise. The only space open to them was up on the stage, and they went up there, pulled the azure curtains down, made nests.

Billy, curled in his azure nest, found himself staring at Cinderella's silver boots under a throne. And then he remembered that his shoes were ruined, that he *needed* boots. He hated to get out of his nest, but he forced himself to do it. He crawled to the boots on all fours, sat, tried them on.

The boots fit perfectly. Billy Pilgrim was Cinderella, and Cinderella was Billy Pilgrim.

Somewhere in there was a lecture on personal hygiene by the head Englishman, and then a free election. At least half the Americans went on snoozing through it all. The Englishman got up on the stage, and he rapped on the arm of a throne with a swagger stick, called, "Lads, lads, lads— can I have your attention, please?" And so on.

What the Englishman said about survival was this: "If you stop taking pride in your appearance, you will very soon die." He said that he had seen several men die in the following way: "They ceased to stand up straight, then ceased to shave or wash, then ceased to get out of bed, then ceased to talk, then died. There is this much to be said for it: it is evidently a very easy and painless way to go." So it goes.

The Englishman said that he, when captured, had made and kept the following vows to himself: To brush his teeth twice a day, to shave once a day, to wash his face and hands before every meal and after going to the latrine, to polish his shoes once a day, to exercise for at least half an hour each morning and then move his bowels, and to look into a mirror frequently, frankly evaluating his appearance, particularly with respect to posture.

Billy Pilgrim heard all this while lying in his nest. He looked not at the Englishman's face but his ankles.

"I *envy* you lads," said the Englishman.

Somebody laughed. Billy wondered what the joke was.

"You lads are leaving this afternoon for Dresden—a beautiful city, I'm told. You won't be cooped up like us. You'll be out where the life is, and the food is certain to be more plentiful than here. If I may inject a personal note: It has been five years now since I have seen a tree or flower or woman or child—or a dog or a cat or a place of entertainment, or a human being doing useful work of any kind.

"You needn't worry about bombs, by the way. Dresden is an open city. It is undefended, and contains no war industries or troop concentrations of any importance."

Somewhere in there, old Edgar Derby was elected head American. The Englishman called for nominations from the floor, and there weren't any. So he nominated Derby, praising him for his maturity and long experience in dealing with people. There were no further nominations, so the nominations were closed.

"All in favor?"

Two or three people said, "Aye."

Then poor old Derby made a speech. He thanked the Englishman for his good advice, said he meant to follow it exactly. He said he was sure that all the other Americans would do the same. He said that his primary responsibility now was to make damn well sure that everybody got home safely.

"Go take a flying fuck at a rolling doughnut," murmured Paul Lazzaro in his azure nest. "Go take a flying fuck at the moon."

The temperature climbed startlingly that day. The noontime was balmy. The Germans brought soup and bread in two-wheeled carts which were pulled by Russians.

The Englishman sent over real coffee and sugar and marmalade and cigarettes and cigars, and the doors of the theater were left open, so the warmth could get in.

The Americans began to feel much better. They were able to hold their food. And then it was time to go to Dresden. The Americans marched fairly stylishly out of the British compound. Billy Pilgrim again led the parade. He had silver boots now, and a muff, and a piece of azure curtain which he wore like a toga. Billy still had a beard. So did poor old Edgar Derby, who was beside him. Derby was imagining letters to home, his lips working tremulously:

Dear Margaret—We are leaving for Dresden today. Don't worry. It will never be bombed. It is an open city. There was an election at noon, and guess what? And so on.

They came to the prison railroad yard again. They had arrived on only two cars. They would depart far more comfortably on four. They saw the dead hobo again. He was frozen stiff in the weeds beside the track. He was in a fetal position, trying even in death to nestle like a spoon with others. There were no others now. He was nestling with thin air and cinders. Somebody had taken his boots. His bare feet were blue and ivory. It was all right, somehow, his being dead. So it goes.

The trip to Dresden was a lark. It took only two hours. Shriveled little bellies were full. Sunlight and mild air came in through the ventilators. There were plenty of smokes from the Englishmen.

The Americans arrived in Dresden at five in the afternoon. The boxcar doors were opened, and the doorways framed the loveliest city that most of the Americans had ever seen. The skyline was intricate and voluptuous and enchanted and absurd. It looked like a Sunday school picture of Heaven to Billy Pilgrim.

Somebody behind him in the boxcar said, "Oz." That was I. That was me. The only other city I'd ever seen was Indianapolis, Indiana.

Every other big city in Germany had been bombed and burned ferociously. Dresden had not suffered so much as a cracked windowpane. Sirens went off every day, screamed like hell, and people went down into cellars and listened to radios there. The planes were always bound for someplace else—Leipzig, Chemnitz, Plauen, places like that. So it goes.

Steam radiators still whistled cheerily in Dresden. Streetcars clanged. Telephones rang and were answered. Lights went on and off when switches were clicked. There were theaters and restaurants. There was a zoo. The principal enterprises of the city were medicine and food-processing and the making of cigarettes.

People were going home from work now in the late afternoon. They were tired.

Eight Dresdeners crossed the steel spaghetti of the railroad yard. They were wearing new uniforms. They had been sworn into the army the day before. They were boys and men past middle age, and two veterans who had been shot to pieces in Russia. Their assignment was to guard one hundred American prisoners of war, who would work as contract labor. A grandfather and his grandson were in the squad. The grandfather was an architect.

The eight were grim as they approached the boxcars containing their wards. They knew what sick and foolish soldiers they themselves appeared to be. One of them actually had an artificial leg, and carried not only a loaded rifle but a cane. Still—they were expected to earn obedience and respect from tall, cocky, murderous American infantrymen who had just come from all the killing at the front.

And then they saw bearded Billy Pilgrim in his blue toga and silver shoes, with his hands in a muff. He looked at least sixty years old. Next to Billy was little Paul Lazzaro with a broken arm. He was fizzing with rabies. Next to Lazzaro was the poor old high school teacher, Edgar Derby, mournfully pregnant with patriotism and middle age and imaginary wisdom. And so on.

The eight ridiculous Dresdeners ascertained that these hundred ridiculous creatures really *were* American fighting men fresh from the front. They smiled, and then they laughed. Their terror evaporated. There was nothing to be afraid of. Here were more crippled human beings, more fools like themselves. Here was light opera.

So out of the gate of the railroad yard and into the streets of Dresden marched the light opera. Billy Pilgrim was the star. He led the parade. Thousands of people were on the sidewalks, going home from work. They were watery and putty-colored, having eaten mostly potatoes during the past two years. They had expected no blessings beyond the mildness of the day. Suddenly—here was fun.

Billy did not meet many of the eyes that found him so entertaining. He was enchanted by the architecture of the city. Merry amoretti wove garlands above windows. Roguish fauns and naked nymphs peeked down at Billy from festooned cornices. Stone monkeys frisked among scrolls and seashells and bamboo.

Billy, with his memories of the future, knew that the city would be smashed to smithereens and then burned—in about thirty more days. He knew, too, that most of the people watching him would soon be dead. So it goes.

And Billy worked his hands in his muff as he marched. His fingertips, working there in the hot darkness of the muff, wanted to know what the two lumps in the lining of the little impresario's coat were. The fingertips got inside the lining. They palpated the lumps, the pea-shaped thing and the horseshoe-shaped thing. The parade had to halt by a busy corner. The traffic light was red.

There at the corner, in the front rank of pedestrians, was a surgeon who had been operating all day. He was a civilian, but his posture was military. He had served in two world wars. The sight of Billy offended him, especially after he learned from the guards that Billy was an American. It seemed to him that Billy was in abominable taste, supposed that Billy had gone to a lot of silly trouble to costume himself just so.

The surgeon spoke English, and he said to Billy, "I take it you find war a very comical thing."

Billy looked at him vaguely. Billy had lost track momentarily of where he was or how he had gotten there. He had no idea that people thought he was clowning. It was Fate, of course, which had costumed him—Fate, and a feeble will to survive.

"Did you expect us to *laugh?*" the surgeon asked him.

The surgeon was demanding some sort of satisfaction. Billy was mystified. Billy wanted to be friendly, to help, if he could, but his resources were meager. His fingers now held the two objects from the lining of the coat. Billy decided to show the surgeon what they were.

"You thought we would enjoy being *mocked?*" the surgeon said. "And do you feel *proud* to represent America as you do?"

Billy withdrew a hand from his muff, held it under the surgeon's nose. On his palm rested a two-carat diamond and a partial denture. The denture was an obscene little artifact—silver and pearl and tangerine. Billy smiled.

The parade pranced, staggered and reeled to the gate of the Dresden slaughterhouse, and then it went inside. The slaughterhouse wasn't a busy place any more. Almost all the hooved animals in Germany had been killed and eaten and excreted by human beings, mostly soldiers. So it goes.

The Americans were taken to the fifth building inside the gate. It was a one-story cement-block cube with sliding doors in front and back. It had been built as a shelter for pigs about to be butchered. Now it was going to serve as a home away from home for one hundred American prisoners of war. There were bunks in there, and two potbellied stoves and a water tap. Behind it was a latrine, which was a one-rail fence with buckets under it.

There was a big number over the door of the building. The number was *five.* Before the Americans could go inside, their only English-speaking guard told them to memorize their simple address, in case they got lost in the big city. Their address was this: "Schlachthof-fünf." *Schlachthof* meant *slaughterhouse. Fünf* was good old *five.*

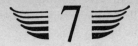

7

Billy Pilgrim got onto a chartered airplane in Ilium twenty-five years after that. He knew it was going to crash, but he didn't want to make a fool of himself by saying so. It was supposed to carry Billy and twenty-eight other optometrists to a convention in Montreal.

His wife, Valencia, was outside, and his father-in-law, Lionel Merble, was strapped to the seat beside him.

Lionel Merble was a machine. Tralfamadorians, of course, say that every creature and plant in the Universe is a machine. It amuses them that so many Earthlings are offended by the idea of being machines.

Outside the plane, the machine named Valencia Merble Pilgrim was eating a Peter Paul Mound Bar and waving bye-bye.

The plane took off without incident. The moment was structured that way. There was a barbershop quartet on board. They were optometrists, too. They called themselves "The Febs," which was an acronym for "Four-eyed Bastards."

When the plane was safely aloft, the machine that was Billy's father-in-law asked the quartet to sing his favorite song. They knew what song he meant, and they sang it, and it went like this:

In my prison cell I sit,
With my britches full of shit,
And my balls are bouncing gently on the floor.
And I see the bloody snag
When she bit me in the bag.
Oh, I'll never fuck a Polack any more.

Billy's father-in-law laughed and laughed at that, and he begged the quartet to sing the other Polish song he liked so much. So they sang a song from the Pennsylvania coal mines that began:

Me and Mike, ve vork in mine.
Holy shit, ve have good time.
Vunce a veek ve get our pay.
Holy shit, no vork next day.

Speaking of people from Poland: Billy Pilgrim accidentally saw a Pole hanged in public, about three days after Billy got to Dresden. Billy just happened to be walking to work with some others shortly after sunrise, and they came to a gallows and a small crowd in front of a soccer stadium. The Pole was a farm laborer who was being hanged for having had sexual intercourse with a German woman. So it goes.

Billy, knowing the plane was going to crash pretty soon, closed his eyes, traveled in time back to 1944. He was back in the forest in Luxembourg again—with the Three Musketeers. Roland Weary was shaking him, bonking his head against a tree. "You guys go on without me," said Billy Pilgrim.

The barbershop quartet on the airplane was singing "Wait Till the Sun Shines, Nelly," when the plane smacked into the top of Sugarbush Mountain in Vermont. Everybody was killed but Billy and the copilot. So it goes.

The people who first got to the crash scene were young

Austrian ski instructors from the famous ski resort below. They spoke to each other in German as they went from body to body. They wore black wind masks with two holes for their eyes and a red topknot. They looked like golliwogs, like white people pretending to be black for the laughs they could get.

Billy had a fractured skull, but he was still conscious. He didn't know where he was. His lips were working, and one of the golliwogs put his ear close to them to hear what might be his dying words.

Billy thought the golliwog had something to do with World War Two, and he whispered to him his address: "Schlachthof-fünf."

Billy was brought down Sugarbush Mountain on a toboggan. The golliwogs controlled it with ropes and yodeled melodiously for right-of-way. Near the bottom, the trail swooped around the pylons of a chair lift. Billy looked up at all the young people in bright elastic clothing and enormous boots and goggles, bombed out of their skulls with snow, swinging through the sky in yellow chairs. He supposed that they were part of an amazing new phase of World War Two. It was all right with him. Everything was pretty much all right with Billy.

He was taken to a small private hospital. A famous brain surgeon came up from Boston and operated on him for three hours. Billy was unconscious for two days after that, and he dreamed millions of things, some of them true. The true things were time-travel.

One of the true things was his first evening in the slaughterhouse. He and poor old Edgar Derby were pushing an empty two-wheeled cart down a dirt lane between empty pens for animals. They were going to a communal kitchen for supper for all. They were guarded by a sixteen-year-old German named Werner Gluck. The axles of the cart were greased with the fat of dead animals. So it goes.

The sun had just gone down, and its afterglow was back-lighting the city, which formed low cliffs around the bucolic void to the idle stockyards. The city was blacked out because bombers might come, so Billy didn't get to see Dresden do one of the most cheerful things a city is capable of doing when the sun goes down, which is to wink its lights on one by one.

There was a broad river to reflect those lights, which would have made their nighttime winkings very pretty indeed. It was the Elbe.

Werner Gluck, the young guard, was a Dresden boy. He had never been in the slaughterhouse before, so he wasn't sure where the kitchen was. He was tall and weak like Billy, might have been a younger brother of his. They were, in fact, distant cousins, something they never found out. Gluck was armed with an incredibly heavy musket, a single-shot museum piece with an octagonal barrel and a smooth bore. He had fixed his bayonet. It was like a long knitting needle. It had no blood gutters.

Gluck led the way to a building that he thought might contain the kitchen, and he opened the sliding door in its side. There wasn't a kitchen in there, though. There was a dressing room adjacent to a communal shower, and there was a lot of steam. In the steam were about thirty teen-age girls with no clothes on. They were German refugees from Breslau, which had been tremendously bombed. They had just arrived in Dresden, too. Dresden was jammed with refugees.

There those girls were with all their private parts bare,

for anybody to see. And there in the doorway were Gluck and Derby and Pilgrim—the childish soldier and the poor old high school teacher and the clown in his toga and silver shoes—staring. The girls screamed. They covered themselves with their hands and turned their backs and so on, and made themselves utterly beautiful.

Werner Gluck, who had never seen a naked woman before, closed the door. Billy had never seen one, either. It was nothing new to Derby.

When the three fools found the communal kitchen, whose main job was to make lunch for workers in the slaughterhouse, everybody had gone home but one woman who had been waiting for them impatiently. She was a war widow. So it goes. She had her hat and coat on. She wanted to go home, too, even though there wasn't anybody there. Her white gloves were laid out side by side on the zinc counter top.

She had two big cans of soup for the Americans. It was simmering over low fires on the gas range. She had stacks of loaves of black bread, too.

She asked Gluck if he wasn't awfully young to be in the army. He admitted that he was.

She asked Edgar Derby if he wasn't awfully old to be in the army. He said he was.

She asked Billy Pilgrim what he was supposed to be. Billy said he didn't know. He was just trying to keep warm.

"All the real soldiers are dead," she said. It was true. So it goes.

Another true thing that Billy saw while he was unconscious in Vermont was the work that he and the others had to do in Dresden during the month before the city was destroyed. They washed windows and swept floors and cleaned lavatories and put jars into boxes and sealed cardboard boxes in a factory that made malt syrup. The syrup was enriched with vitamins and minerals. The syrup was for pregnant women.

The syrup tasted like thin honey laced with hickory smoke, and everybody who worked in the factory secretly spooned it all day long. They weren't pregnant, but they needed vitamins and minerals, too. Billy didn't spoon syrup on his first day at work, but lots of other Americans did.

Billy spooned it on his second day. There were spoons hidden all over the factory, on rafters, in drawers, behind radiators, and so on. They had been hidden in haste by persons who had been spooning syrup, who had heard somebody else coming. Spooning was a crime.

On his second day, Billy was cleaning behind a radiator, and he found a spoon. To his back was a vat of syrup that was cooling. The only other person who could see Billy and his spoon was poor old Edgar Derby, who was washing a window outside. The spoon was a tablespoon. Billy thrust it into the vat, turned it around and around, making a gooey lollipop. He thrust it into his mouth.

A moment went by, and then every cell in Billy's body shook him with ravenous gratitude and applause.

There were diffident raps on the factory window. Derby was out there, having seen all. He wanted some syrup, too.

So Billy made a lollipop for him. He opened the window. He stuck the lollipop into poor old Derby's gaping mouth. A moment passed, and then Derby burst into tears. Billy closed the window and hid the sticky spoon. Somebody was coming.

[138]

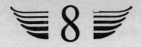

8

The Americans in the slaughterhouse had a very interesting visitor two days before Dresden was destroyed. He was Howard W. Campbell, Jr., an American who had become a Nazi. Campbell was the one who had written the monograph about the shabby behavior of American prisoners of war. He wasn't doing more research about prisoners now. He had come to the slaughterhouse to recruit men for a German military unit called "The Free American Corps." Campbell was the inventor and commander of the unit, which was supposed to fight only on the Russian front.

Campbell was an ordinary-looking man, but he was extravagantly costumed in a uniform of his own design. He wore a white ten-gallon hat and black cowboy boots decorated with swastikas and stars. He was sheathed in a blue body stocking which had yellow stripes running from his armpits to his ankles. His shoulder patch was a silhouette of Abraham Lincoln's profile on a field of pale green. He had a broad armband which was red, with a blue swastika in a circle of white.

He was explaining this armband now in the cement-block hog barn.

Billy Pilgrim had a boiling case of heartburn, since he had been spooning malt syrup all day long at work. The heartburn brought tears to his eyes, so that his image of Campbell was distorted by jiggling lenses of salt water.

"Blue is for the American sky," Campbell was saying. "White is for the race that pioneered the continent, drained the swamps and cleared the forests and built the roads and bridges. Red is for the blood of American patriots which was shed so gladly in years gone by."

Campbell's audience was sleepy. It had worked hard at the syrup factory, and then it had marched a long way home in the cold. It was skinny and hollow-eyed. Its skins were beginning to blossom with small sores. So were its mouths and throats and intestines. The malt syrup it spooned at the factory contained only a few of the vitamins and minerals every Earthling needs.

Campbell offered the Americans food now, steaks and mashed potatoes and gravy and mince pie, if they would join the Free American Corps. "Once the Russians are defeated," he went on, "you will be repatriated through Switzerland."

There was no response.

"You're going to have to fight the Communists sooner or later," said Campbell. "Why not get it over with now?"

And then it developed that Campbell was not going to go unanswered after all. Poor old Derby, the doomed high school teacher, lumbered to his feet for what was probably the finest moment in his life. There are almost no characters in this story, and almost no dramatic confrontations, because most of the people in it are so sick and so much the listless playthings of enormous forces. One of the main effects of war, after all, is that people are discouraged from being characters. But old Derby was a character now.

His stance was that of a punch-drunk fighter. His head was down. His fists were out front, waiting for information and battle plan. Derby raised his head, called Campbell a snake. He corrected that. He said that snakes couldn't help being snakes, and that Campbell, who *could* help being what he was, was something much lower than a snake or a rat—or even a blood-filled tick.

Campbell smiled.

Derby spoke movingly of the American form of government, with freedom and justice and opportunities and fair play for all. He said there wasn't a man there who wouldn't gladly die for those ideals.

He spoke of the brotherhood between the American and the Russian people, and how those two nations were going to crush the disease of Nazism, which wanted to infect the whole world.

The air-raid sirens of Dresden howled mournfully.

The Americans and their guards and Campbell took shelter in an echoing meat locker which was hollowed in living rock under the slaughterhouse. There was an iron staircase with iron doors at the top and bottom.

Down in the locker were a few cattle and sheep and pigs and horses hanging from iron hooks. So it goes. The locker had empty hooks for thousands more. It was naturally cool. There was no refrigeration. There was candlelight. The locker was whitewashed and smelled of carbolic acid. There were benches along a wall. The Americans went to these, brushing away flakes of whitewash before they sat down.

Howard W. Campbell, Jr., remained standing, like the

guards. He talked to the guards in excellent German. He had written many popular German plays and poems in his time, and had married a famous German actress named Resi North. She was dead now, had been killed while entertaining troops in the Crimea. So it goes.

Nothing happened that night. It was the next night that about one hundred and thirty thousand people in Dresden would die. So it goes. Billy dozed in the meat locker. He found himself engaged again, word for word, gesture for gesture, in the argument with his daughter with which this tale began.

"Father," she said, "What are we going to *do* with you?" And so on. "You know who I could just kill?" she asked.

"*Who* could you kill?" said Billy.

"That Kilgore Trout."

Kilgore Trout was and is a science-fiction writer, of course. Billy has not only read dozens of books by Trout— he has also become Trout's friend, to the extent that anyone can become a friend of Trout, who is a bitter man.

Trout lives in a rented basement in Ilium, about two miles from Billy's nice white home. He himself has no idea how many novels he has written—possibly seventy-five of the things. Not one of them has made money. So Trout keeps body and soul together as a circulation man for the *Ilium Gazette,* manages newspaper delivery boys, bullies and flatters and cheats little kids.

Billy met him for the first time in 1964. Billy drove his Cadillac down a back alley in Ilium, and he found his way blocked by dozens of boys and their bicycles. A meeting was in progress. The boys were harangued by a man in a full beard. He was cowardly and dangerous, and obviously very good at his job. Trout was sixty-two years old back then. He was telling the kids to get off their dead butts and get their daily customers to subscribe to the fucking Sunday edition, too. He said that whoever sold the most Sunday subscriptions during the next two months would get a free trip for himself and his parents to Martha's fucking Vineyard for a week, all expenses paid.

And so on.

One of the newspaper boys was actually a newspaper *girl*. She was electrified.

Trout's paranoid face was terribly familiar to Billy, who had seen it on the jackets of so many books. But, coming upon that face suddenly in a home-town alley, Billy could not guess why the face was familiar. Billy thought maybe he had known this cracked messiah in Dresden somewhere. Trout certainly looked like a prisoner of war.

And then the newspaper girl held up her hand. "Mr. Trout—" she said, "if I win, can I take my sister, too?"

"Hell no," said Kilgore Trout. "You think money grows on *trees?*"

Trout, incidentally, had written a book about a money tree. It had twenty-dollar bills for leaves. Its flowers were government bonds. Its fruit was diamonds. It attracted human beings who killed each other around the roots and made very good fertilizer.

So it goes.

Billy Pilgrim parked his Cadillac in the alley, and waited for the meeting to end. When the meeting broke up, there was still one boy Trout had to deal with. The boy wanted to quit because the work was so hard and the hours were so long and the pay was so small. Trout was concerned, because, if the boy really quit, Trout would have to deliver the boy's route himself, until he could find another sucker.

"What are you?" Trout asked the boy scornfully. "Some kind of gutless wonder?"

This, too, was the title of a book by Trout, *The Gutless Wonder*. It was about a robot who had bad breath, who became popular after his halitosis was cured. But what made the story remarkable, since it was written in 1932, was that it predicted the widespread use of burning jellied gasoline on human beings.

It was dropped on them from airplanes. Robots did the dropping. They had no conscience, and no circuits which would allow them to imagine what was happening to the people on the ground.

Trout's leading robot looked like a human being, and could talk and dance and so on, and go out with girls. And nobody held it against him that he dropped jellied gasoline on people. But they found his halitosis unforgivable. But then he cleared that up, and he was welcomed to the human race.

Trout lost his argument with the boy who wanted to quit. He told the boy about all the millionaires who had carried newspapers as boys, and the boy replied: "Yeah—but I bet they quit after a week, it's *such* a royal screwing."

And the boy left his full newspaper bag at Trout's feet, with the customer book on top. It was up to Trout to deliver these papers. He didn't have a car. He didn't even have a bicycle, and he was scared to death of dogs.

Somewhere a big dog barked.

As Trout lugubriously slung the bag from his shoulder, Billy Pilgrim approached him. "Mr. Trout—?"

"Yes?"

"Are—are you *Kilgore* Trout?"

"Yes." Trout supposed that Billy had some complaint about the way his newspapers were being delivered. He did not think of himself as a writer for the simple reason that the world had never allowed him to think of himself in this way.

"The—the writer?" said Billy.

"The what?"

Billy was certain that he had made a mistake. "There's a writer named Kilgore Trout."

"There *is?*" Trout looked foolish and dazed.

"You never heard of him?"

Trout shook his head. "Nobody—nobody ever did."

Billy helped Trout deliver his papers, driving him from house to house in the Cadillac. Billy was the responsible one, finding the houses, checking them off. Trout's mind was blown. He had never met a fan before, and Billy was such an *avid* fan.

Trout told him that he had never seen a book of his advertised, reviewed, or on sale. "All these years," he said, "I've been opening the window and making love to the world."

"You must surely have gotten letters," said Billy. "I've felt like writing you letters many times."

Trout held up a single finger. "One."

"Was it *enthusiastic?*"

"It was *insane*. The writer said I should be President of the World."

It turned out that the person who had written this letter

was Eliot Rosewater, Billy's friend in the veterans' hospital near Lake Placid. Billy told Trout about Rosewater.

"My God—I thought he was about fourteen years old," said Trout.

"A full grown man—a captain in the war."

"He *writes* like a fourteen-year-old," said Kilgore Trout.

Billy invited Trout to his eighteenth wedding anniversary which was only two days hence. Now the party was in progress.

Trout was in Billy's dining room, gobbling canapés. He was talking with a mouthful of Philadelphia cream cheese and salmon roe to an optometrist's wife. Everybody at the party was associated with optometry in some way, except Trout. And he alone was without glasses. He was making a great hit. Everybody was thrilled to have a real author at the party, even though they had never read his books.

Trout was talking to a Maggie White, who had given up being a dental assistant to become a homemaker for an optometrist. She was very pretty. The last book she had read was *Ivanhoe*.

Billy Pilgrim stood nearby, listening. He was palpating something in his pocket. It was a present he was about to give his wife, a white satin box containing a star sapphire cocktail ring. The ring was worth eight hundred dollars.

The adulation that Trout was receiving, mindless and illiterate as it was, affected Trout like marijuana. He was happy and loud and impudent.

"I'm afraid I don't read as much as I *ought* to," said Maggie.

"We're all afraid of something," Trout replied. "I'm afraid of cancer and rats and Doberman pinschers."

"I should know, but I don't, so I have to ask," said Maggie, "what's the most famous thing you ever wrote?"

"It was about a funeral for a great French chef."

"That sounds interesting."

"All the great chefs in the world are there. It's a beautiful ceremony." Trout was making this up as he went along. "Just before the casket is closed, the mourners sprinkle parsley and paprika on the deceased." So it goes.

"Did that really *happen?*" said Maggie White. She was a dull person, but a sensational invitation to make babies. Men looked at her and wanted to fill her up with babies right away. She hadn't had even one baby yet. She used birth control.

"Of course it happened," Trout told her. "If I wrote something that hadn't really happened, and I tried to sell it, I could go to jail. That's *fraud.*"

Maggie believed him. "I'd never thought about that before."

"Think about it now."

"It's like advertising. You have to tell the truth in advertising, or you get in trouble."

"Exactly. The same body of law applies."

"Do you think you might put *us* in a book sometime?"

"I put everything that happens to me in books."

"I guess I better be careful what I say."

"That's right. And I'm not the only one who's listening. God is listening, too. And on Judgment Day he's going to tell you all the things you said and did. If it turns out they're bad things instead of good things, that's too bad for you, because you'll burn forever and ever. The burning never stops hurting."

Poor Maggie turned gray. She believed *that,* too, and was petrified.

Kilgore Trout laughed uproariously. A salmon egg flew out of his mouth and landed in Maggie's cleavage.

Now an optometrist called for attention. He proposed a toast to Billy and Valencia, whose anniversary it was. According to plan, the barbershop quartet of optometrists, "The Febs," sang while people drank and Billy and Valencia put their arms around each other, just glowed. Everybody's eyes were shining. The song was "That Old Gang of Mine."

Gee, that song went, *but I'd give the world to see that old gang of mine.* And so on. A little later it said, *So long forever, old fellows and gals, so long forever old sweethearts and pals—God bless 'em—*And so on.

Unexpectedly, Billy Pilgrim found himself upset by the song and the occasion. He had never had an old gang, old sweethearts and pals, but he missed one anyway, as the quartet made slow, agonized experiments with chords—chords intentionally sour, sourer still, unbearably sour, and then a chord that was suffocatingly sweet, and then some sour ones again. Billy had powerful psychosomatic responses to the changing chords. His mouth filled with the taste of lemonade, and his face became grotesque, as though he really were being stretched on the torture engine called the *rack.*

He looked so peculiar that several people commented on it solicitously when the song was done. They thought he might have been having a heart attack, and Billy seemed to confirm this by going to a chair and sitting down haggardly.

There was silence.

"Oh my God," said Valencia, leaning over him, "Billy—are you all right?"

"Yes."

"You look so awful."

"Really—I'm O.K." And he was, too, except that he could find no explanation for why the song had affected him so grotesquely. He had supposed for years that he had no secrets from himself. Here was proof that he had a great big secret somewhere inside, and he could not imagine what it was.

People drifted away now, seeing the color return to Billy's cheeks, seeing him smile. Valencia stayed with him, and Kilgore Trout, who had been on the fringe of the crowd, came closer, interested, shrewd.

"You looked as though you'd seen a *ghost,*" said Valencia.

"No," said Billy. He hadn't seen anything but what was really before him—the faces of the four singers, those four ordinary men, cow-eyed and mindless and anguished as they went from sweetness to sourness to sweetness again.

"Can I make a guess?" said Kilgore Trout. "You saw through a *time window.*"

"A what?" said Valencia.

"He suddenly saw the past or the future. Am I right?"

"No," said Billy Pilgrim. He got up, put a hand into his pocket, found the box containing the ring in there. He took out the box, gave it absently to Valencia. He had meant to give it to her at the end of the song, while everybody was watching. Only Kilgore Trout was there to see.

"For me?" said Valencia.

"Yes."

"Oh my God," she said. Then she said it louder, so other people heard. They gathered around, and she opened it, and she almost screamed when she saw the sapphire with a star in it. "Oh, my God," she said. She gave Billy a big kiss. She said, "Thank you, thank you, thank you."

There was a lot of talk about what wonderful jewelry Billy had given to Valencia over the years. "My God—" said Maggie White, "she's already got the biggest diamond I ever saw outside of a movie." She was talking about the diamond Billy had brought back from the war.

The partial denture he had found inside his little impresario's coat, incidentally, was in his cufflinks box in his dresser drawer. Billy had a wonderful collection of cufflinks. It was the custom of the family to give him cufflinks on every Father's Day. He was wearing Father's Day cufflinks now. They had cost over one hundred dollars. They were made out of ancient Roman coins. He had one pair of cufflinks upstairs which were little roulette wheels that really worked. He had another pair which had a real thermometer in one and a real compass in the other.

Billy now moved about the party—outwardly normal. Kilgore Trout was shadowing him, keen to know what Billy had suspected or seen. Most of Trout's novels, after all, dealt with time warps and extrasensory perception and other unexpected things. Trout believed in things like that, was greedy to have their existence proved.

"You ever put a full-length mirror on the floor, and then have a dog stand on it?" Trout asked Billy.

"No."

"The dog will look down, and all of a sudden he'll realize there's nothing under him. He thinks he's standing on thin air. He'll jump a *mile*."

"He *will?*"

"That's how *you* looked—as though you all of a sudden realized you were standing on thin air."

The barbershop quartet sang again. Billy was emotionally racked again. The experience was *definitely* associated with those four men and not what they sang.

Here is what they sang, while Billy was pulled apart inside:

> 'Leven cent cotton, forty cent meat,
> How in the world can a poor man eat?
> Pray for the sunshine, 'cause it will rain.
> Things gettin' worse, drivin' all insane;
> Built a nice bar, painted it brown;
> Lightnin' came along and burnt it down:
> No use talkin', any man's beat,
> With 'leven cent cotton and forty cent meat.
> 'Leven cent cotton, a car-load of tax,
> The load's too heavy for our poor backs . . .

And so on.

Billy fled upstairs in his nice white home.

Trout would have come upstairs with him if Billy hadn't told him not to. Then Billy went into the upstairs bathroom, which was dark. He closed and locked the door. He left it dark, and gradually became aware that he was not alone. His son was in there.

"Dad—?" his son said in the dark. Robert, the future Green Beret, was seventeen then. Billy liked him, but didn't know him very well. Billy couldn't help suspecting that there wasn't much *to* know about Robert.

Billy flicked on the light. Robert was sitting on the toilet with his pajama bottoms around his ankles. He was wearing an electric guitar, slung around his neck on a strap. He had just bought the guitar that day. He couldn't play it yet and, in fact, never learned to play it. It was a nacreous pink.

"Hello, son," said Billy Pilgrim.

Billy went into his bedroom, even though there were guests to be entertained downstairs. He lay down on his bed, turned on the Magic Fingers. The mattress trembled, drove a dog out from under the bed. The dog was Spot. Good old Spot was still alive in those days. Spot lay down again in a corner.

Billy thought hard about the effect the quartet had had on him, and then found an association with an experience he had had long ago. He did not travel in time to the experience. He remembered it shimmeringly—as follows:

He was down in the meat locker on the night that Dresden was destroyed. There were sounds like giant footsteps above. Those were sticks of high-explosive bombs. The giants walked and walked. The meat locker was a very safe shelter. All that happened down there was an occasional shower of calcimine. The Americans and four of their guards and a few dressed carcasses were down there, and nobody else. The rest of the guards had, before the raid began, gone to the comforts of their own homes in Dresden. They were all being killed with their families.

So it goes.

The girls that Billy had seen naked were all being killed, too, in a much shallower shelter in another part of the stockyards.

So it goes.

A guard would go to the head of the stairs every so often to see what it was like outside, then he would come down and whisper to the other guards. There was a fire-storm out there. Dresden was one big flame. The one flame ate everything organic, everything that would burn.

It wasn't safe to come out of the shelter until noon the next day. When the Americans and their guards did come out, the sky was black with smoke. The sun was an angry little pinhead. Dresden was like the moon now, nothing but minerals. The stones were hot. Everybody else in the neighborhood was dead.

So it goes.

The guards drew together instinctively, rolled their eyes. They experimented with one expression and then another, said nothing, though their mouths were often open. They looked like a silent film of a barbershop quartet.

"So long forever," they might have been singing, "old fellows and pals; So long forever, old sweethearts and pals—God bless 'em—"

"Tell me a story," Montana Wildhack said to Billy Pilgrim in the Tralfamadorian zoo one time. They were in bed side by side. They had privacy. The canopy covered the dome. Montana was six months pregnant now, big and rosy, lazily demanding small favors from Billy from time to time. She couldn't send Billy out for ice cream or strawberries, since the atmosphere outside the dome was cyanide, and the nearest strawberries and ice cream were millions of light years away.

She could send him to the refrigerator, which was decorated with the blank couple on the bicycle built for two— or, as now, she could wheedle, "Tell me a story, Billy boy."

"Dresden was destroyed on the night of February 13, 1945," Billy Pilgrim began. "We came out of our shelter the next day." He told Montana about the four guards who, in their astonishment and grief, resembled a barbershop quartet. He told her about the stockyards with all the fenceposts gone, with roofs and windows gone—told her about seeing little logs lying around. These were people who had been caught in the fire storm. So it goes.

Billy told her what had happened to the buildings that used to form cliffs around the stockyards. They had collapsed. Their wood had been consumed, and their stones had crashed down, had tumbled against one another until they locked at last in low and graceful curves.

"It was like the moon," said Billy Pilgrim.

The guards told the Americans to form in ranks of four, which they did. Then they had them march back to the hog barn which had been their home. Its walls still stood, but its windows and roof were gone, and there was nothing inside but ashes and dollops of melted glass. It was realized then that there was no food or water, and that the survivors, if they were going to continue to survive, were going to have to climb over curve after curve on the face of the moon.

Which they did.

The curves were smooth only when seen from a distance. The people climbing them learned that they were treacherous, jagged things—hot to the touch, often unstable—eager, should certain important rocks be disturbed, to tumble some more, to form lower, more solid curves.

Nobody talked much as the expedition crossed the moon. There was nothing appropriate to say. One thing was clear: Absolutely everybody in the city was supposed to be dead, regardless of what they were, and that anybody that moved in it represented a flaw in the design. There were to be no moon men at all.

American fighter planes came in under the smoke to see if anything was moving. They saw Billy and the rest moving down there. The planes sprayed them with machine-gun bullets, but the bullets missed. Then they saw some other people moving down by the riverside and they shot at them. They hit some of them. So it goes.

The idea was to hasten the end of the war.

Billy's story ended very curiously in a suburb untouched by fire and explosions. The guards and the Americans came at nightfall to an inn which was open for business. There was candlelight. There were fires in three fireplaces downstairs. There were empty tables and chairs waiting for anyone who might come, and empty beds with covers turned down upstairs.

There was a blind innkeeper and his sighted wife, who was the cook, and their two young daughters, who worked as waitresses and maids. This family knew that Dresden was gone. Those with eyes had seen it burn and burn, understood that they were on the edge of a desert now. Still—they had opened for business, had polished the glasses and wound the clocks and stirred the fires, and waited and waited to see who would come.

There was no great flow of refugees from Dresden. The clocks ticked on, the fires crackled, the translucent candles dripped. And then there was a knock on the door, and in came four guards and one hundred American prisoners of war.

The innkeeper asked the guards if they had come from the city.

"Yes."

"Are there more people coming?"

And the guards said that, on the difficult route they had chosen, they had not seen another living soul.

The blind innkeeper said that the Americans could sleep in his stable that night, and he gave them soup and ersatz coffee and a little beer. Then he came out to the stable to listen to them bedding down in the straw.

"Good night, Americans," he said in German. "Sleep well."

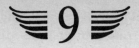

9

Here is how Billy Pilgrim lost his wife, Valencia.

He was unconscious in the hospital in Vermont, after the airplane crashed on Sugarbush Mountain, and Valencia, having heard about the crash, was driving from Ilium to the hospital in the family Cadillac El Dorado Coupe de Ville. Valencia was hysterical, because she had been told frankly that Billy might die, or that, if he lived, he might be a vegetable.

Valencia adored Billy. She was crying and yelping so hard as she drove that she missed the correct turnoff from the throughway. She applied her power brakes, and a Mercedes slammed into her from behind. Nobody was hurt, thank God, because both drivers were wearing seat belts. Thank God, thank God. The Mercedes lost only a headlight. But the rear end of the Cadillac was a body-and-fender man's wet dream. The trunk and fenders were collapsed. The gaping trunk looked like the mouth of a village idiot who was explaining that he didn't know anything about anything. The fenders shrugged. The bumper was at a high port arms. "Reagan for President!" a sticker on the bumper said. The back window was veined with cracks. The exhaust system rested on the pavement.

The driver of the Mercedes got out and went to Valencia, to find out if she was all right. She blabbed hysterically about Billy and the airplane crash, and then she put her car in gear and crossed the median divider, leaving her exhaust system behind.

When she arrived at the hospital, people rushed to the windows to see what all the noise was. The Cadillac, with both mufflers gone, sounded like a heavy bomber coming in on a wing and a prayer. Valencia turned off the engine, but then she slumped against the steering wheel, and the horn brayed steadily. A doctor and a nurse ran out to find out what the trouble was. Poor Valencia was unconscious, overcome by carbon monoxide. She was a heavenly azure.

One hour later she was dead. So it goes.

Billy knew nothing about it. He dreamed on, and traveled in time and so forth. The hospital was so crowded that Billy couldn't have a room to himself. He shared a room with a Harvard history professor named Bertram Copeland Rumfoord. Rumfoord didn't have to look at Billy, because Billy was surrounded by white linen screens on rubber wheels. But Rumfoord could hear Billy talking to himself from time to time.

Rumfoord's left leg was in traction. He had broken it while skiing. He was seventy years old, but had the body and spirit of a man half that age. He had been honeymooning with his fifth wife when he broke his leg. Her name was Lily. Lily was twenty-three.

Just about the time poor Valencia was pronounced dead, Lily came into Billy's and Rumfoord's room with an armload of books. Rumfoord had sent her down to Boston to get them. He was working on a one-volume history of the United States Army Air Corps in World War Two. The books were about bombings and sky battles that had happened before Lily was even *born*.

"You guys go on without me," said Billy Pilgrim deliriously, as pretty little Lily came in. She had been an a-go-go girl when Rumfoord saw her and resolved to make her his own. She was a high school dropout. Her I.Q. was 103. "He *scares* me," she whispered to her husband about Billy Pilgrim.

"He bores the *hell* out of *me!*" Rumfoord replied boomingly. "All he does in his sleep is quit and surrender and apologize and ask to be left alone." Rumfoord was a retired brigadier general in the Air Force Reserve, the official Air Force Historian, a full professor, the author of twenty-six books, a multimillionaire since birth, and one of the great competitive sailors of all time. His most popular book was about sex and strenuous athletics for men over sixty-five. Now he quoted Theodore Roosevelt, whom he resembled a lot:

" 'I could carve a better man out of a banana.' "

One of the things Rumfoord had told Lily to get in Boston was a copy of President Harry S. Truman's announcement to the world that an atomic bomb had been dropped on Hiroshima. She had a Xerox of it, and Rumfoord asked her if she had read it.

"No." She didn't read well, which was one of the reasons she had dropped out of high school.

Rumfoord ordered her to sit down and read the Truman statement now. He didn't know that she couldn't read much. He knew very little about her, except that she was one more public demonstration that he was a superman.

So Lily sat down and pretended to read the Truman thing, which went like this:

Sixteen hours ago an American airplane dropped one bomb on Hiroshima, an important Japanese Army base. That bomb had more power than 20,000 tons of T. N. T. It had more than two thousand times the blast power of the British "Grand Slam," which is the largest bomb ever yet used in the history of warfare.

The Japanese began the war from the air at Pearl Harbor. They have been repaid many-fold. And the end is not yet. With this bomb we have now added a new and revolutionary increase in destruction to supplement the growing power of our armed forces. In their present form these bombs are now in production, and even more powerful forms are in development.

It is an atomic bomb. It is a harnessing of the basic power of the universe. The force from which the sun draws its power has been loosed against those who brought war to the Far East.

Before 1939, it was the accepted belief of scientists that it was theoretically possible to release atomic energy. But nobody knew any practical method of doing it. By 1942, however, we knew that the Germans were working feverishly to find a way to add atomic energy to all the other engines of war with which they hoped to enslave the world. But they failed. We may be grateful to Providence that the Germans got the V-1's and V-2's late and in limited quantities and even more grateful that they did not get the atomic bomb at all.

The battle of the laboratories held fateful risks for us as well as the battles of the air, land, and sea, and we have now won the battle of the laboratories as we have won the other battles.

We are now prepared to obliterate more rapidly and

completely every productive enterprise the Japanese have above ground in any city, said Harry Truman. *We shall destroy their docks, their factories, and their communications. Let there be no mistake; we shall completely destroy Japan's power to make war. It was to spare—*

And so on.

One of the books that Lily had brought Rumfoord was *The Destruction of Dresden,* by an Englishman named David Irving. It was an American edition, published by Holt, Rinehart and Winston in 1964. What Rumfoord wanted from it were portions of the forewords by his friends Ira C. Eaker, Lieutenant General, U.S.A.F., retired, and British Air Marshal Sir Robert Saundby, K.C.B., K.B.E., M.C., D.F.C., A.F.C.

I find it difficult to understand Englishmen or Americans who weep about enemy civilians who were killed but who have not shed a tear for our gallant crews lost in combat with a cruel enemy, wrote his friend General Eaker in part. *I think it would have been well for Mr. Irving to have remembered, when he was drawing the frightful picture of the civilians killed at Dresden, that V-1's and V-2's were at that very time falling on England, killing civilian men, women, and children indiscriminately, as they were designed and launched to do. It might be well to remember Buchenwald and Coventry, too.*

Eaker's foreword ended this way:

I deeply regret that British and U.S. bombers killed 135,000 people in the attack on Dresden, but I remember who started the last war and I regret even more the loss of more than 5,000,000 Allied lives in the necessary effort to completely defeat and utterly destroy nazism.

So it goes.

What Air Marshal Saundby said, among other things, was this:

That the bombing of Dresden was a great tragedy none can deny. That it was really a military necessity few, after reading this book, will believe. It was one of those terrible things that sometimes happen in wartime, brought about by an unfortunate combination of circumstances. Those who approved it were neither wicked nor cruel, though it may well be that they were too remote from the harsh realities of war to understand fully the appalling destructive power of air bombardment in the spring of 1945.

The advocates of nuclear disarmament seem to believe that, if they could achieve their aim, war would become tolerable and decent. They would do well to read this book and ponder the fate of Dresden, where 135,000 people died as the result of an air attack with conventional weapons. On the night of March 9th, 1945, an air attack on Tokyo by American heavy bombers, using incendiary and high explosive bombs, caused the death of 83,793 people. The atom bomb dropped on Hiroshima killed 71,379 people.

So it goes.

"If you're ever in Cody, Wyoming," said Billy Pilgrim behind his white linen screens, "just ask for Wild Bob."

Lily Rumfoord shuddered, went on pretending to read the Harry Truman thing.

Billy's daughter Barbara came in later that day. She was all doped up, had the same glassy-eyed look that poor old Edgar Derby wore just before he was shot in Dresden. Doctors had given her pills so she could continue to function, even though her father was broken and her mother was dead.

So it goes.

She was accompanied by a doctor and a nurse. Her brother Robert was flying home from a battlefield in Vietnam. "Daddy—" she said tentatively. "Daddy—?"

But Billy was ten years away, back in 1958. He was examining the eyes of a young male Mongolian idiot in order to prescribe corrective lenses. The idiot's mother was there, acting as an interpreter.

"How many dots do you see?" Billy Pilgrim asked him.

And then Billy traveled in time to when he was sixteen years old, in the waiting room of a doctor. Billy had an infected thumb. There was only one other patient waiting—an old, old man. The old man was in agony because of gas. He farted tremendously, and then he belched.

"Excuse me," he said to Billy. Then he did it again. "Oh God—" he said, "I knew it was going to be bad getting old." He shook his head. "I didn't know it was going to be *this* bad."

Billy Pilgrim opened his eyes in the hospital in Vermont, did not know where he was. Watching him was his son Robert. Robert was wearing the uniform of the famous Green Berets. Robert's hair was short, was wheat-colored bristles. Robert was clean and neat. He was decorated with a Purple Heart and a Silver Star and a Bronze Star with two clusters.

This was a boy who had flunked out of high school, who had been an alcoholic at sixteen, who had run with a rotten bunch of kids, who had been arrested for tipping over hundreds of tombstones in a Catholic cemetery one time. He was all straightened out now. His posture was wonderful and his shoes were shined and his trousers were pressed, and he was a leader of men.

"Dad—?"

Billy Pilgrim closed his eyes again.

Billy had to miss his wife's funeral because he was still so sick. He was conscious, though, while Valencia was being put into the ground in Ilium. Billy hadn't said much since regaining consciousness, hadn't responded very elaborately to the news of Valencia's death and Robert's coming home from the war and so on—so it was generally believed that he was a vegetable. There was talk of performing an operation on him later, one which might improve the circulation of blood to his brain.

Actually, Billy's outward listlessness was a screen. The listlessness concealed a mind which was fizzing and flashing thrillingly. It was preparing letters and lectures about the flying saucers, the negligibility of death, and the true nature of time.

Professor Rumfoord said frightful things about Billy within Billy's hearing, confident that Billy no longer had any brain at all. "Why don't they let him *die?*" he asked Lily.

"I don't know," she said.

"That's not a human being anymore. Doctors are for human beings. They should turn him over to a veterinarian or a tree surgeon. *They'd* know what to do. Look at him! That's life, according to the medical profession. Isn't life wonderful?"

"I don't know," said Lily.

Rumfoord talked to Lily about the bombing of Dresden one time, and Billy heard it all. Rumfoord had a problem about Dresden. His one-volume history of the Army Air Force in World War Two was supposed to be a readable condensation of the twenty-seven-volume *Official History of the Army Air Force in World War Two*. The thing was, though, there was almost nothing in the twenty-seven volumes about the Dresden raid, even though it had been such a howling success. The extent of the success had been kept a secret for many years after the war—a secret from the American people. It was no secret from the Germans, of course, or from the Russians, who occupied Dresden after the war, who are in Dresden still.

"Americans have finally heard about Dresden," said Rumfoord, twenty-three years after the raid. "A lot of them know now how much worse it was than Hiroshima. So I've got to put something about it in my book. From the official Air Force standpoint, it'll all be new."

"Why would they keep it a secret so long?" said Lily.

"For fear that a lot of bleeding hearts," said Rumfoord, "might not think it was such a wonderful thing to do."

It was now that Billy Pilgrim spoke up intelligently. "I was there," he said.

It was difficult for Rumfoord to take Billy seriously, since Rumfoord had so long considered Billy a repulsive non-person who would be much better off dead. Now, with Billy speaking clearly and to the point, Rumfoord's ears wanted to treat the words as a foreign language that was not worth learning. "What did he say?" said Rumfoord.

Lily had to serve as an interpreter. "He said he was there," she explained.

"He was where?"

"I don't know," said Lily. "Where were you?" she asked Billy.

"Dresden," said Billy.

"Dresden," Lily told Rumfoord.

"He's simply echoing things we say," said Rumfoord.

"Oh," said Lily.

"He's got echolalia now."

"Oh."

Echolalia is a mental disease which makes people immediately repeat things that well people around them say. But Billy didn't really have it. Rumfoord simply insisted, for his own comfort, that Billy had it. Rumfoord was thinking in a military manner: that an inconvenient person, one whose death he wished for very much, for practical reasons, was suffering from a repulsive disease.

Rumfoord went on insisting for several hours that Billy had echolalia—told nurses and a doctor that Billy had echolalia now. Some experiments were performed on Billy. Doctors and nurses tried to get Billy to echo something, but Billy wouldn't make a sound for them.

"He isn't doing it now," said Rumfoord peevishly. "The minute you go away, he'll start doing it again."

Nobody took Rumfoord's diagnosis seriously. The staff thought Rumfoord was a hateful old man, conceited and cruel. He often said to them, in one way or another, that people who were weak deserved to die. Whereas the staff, of course, was devoted to the idea that weak people should be helped as much as possible, that nobody should die.

There in the hospital, Billy was having an adventure very common among people without power in time of war: He was trying to prove to a willfully deaf and blind enemy that he was interesting to hear and see. He kept silent until the lights went out at night, and then, when there had been a long period of silence containing nothing to echo, he said to Rumfoord, "I was in Dresden when it was bombed. I was a prisoner of war."

Rumfoord sighed impatiently.

"Word of honor," said Billy Pilgrim. "Do you believe me?"

"Must we talk about it now?" said Rumfoord. He had heard. He didn't believe.

"We don't ever have to talk about it," said Billy. "I just want you to know: I was there."

Nothing more was said about Dresden that night, and Billy closed his eyes, traveled in time to a May afternoon, two days after the end of the Second World War in Europe. Billy and five other American prisoners were riding in a coffin-shaped green wagon, which they had found abandoned, complete with two horses, in a suburb of Dresden. Now they were being drawn by the clop-clop-clopping horses down narrow lanes which had been cleared through the moonlike ruins. They were going back to the slaughterhouse for souvenirs of the war. Billy was reminded of the sounds of milkmen's horses early in the morning in Ilium, when he was a boy.

Billy sat in the back of the jiggling coffin. His head was tilted back and his nostrils were flaring. He was happy. He was warm. There was food in the wagon, and wine—and a camera, and a stamp collection, and a stuffed owl, and a mantel clock that ran on changes of barometric pressure. The Americans had gone into empty houses in the suburb where they had been imprisoned, and they had taken these and many other things.

The owners, hearing that the Russians were coming, killing and robbing and raping and burning, had fled.

But the Russians hadn't come yet, even two days after the war. It was peaceful in the ruins. Billy saw only one other person on the way to the slaughterhouse. It was an old man pushing a baby buggy. In the buggy were pots and cups and an umbrella frame, and other things he had found.

Billy stayed in the wagon when it reached the slaughter-house, sunning himself. The others went looking for souvenirs. Later on in life, the Tralfamadorians would advise Billy to concentrate on the happy moments of his life, and to ignore the unhappy ones—to stare only at pretty things as eternity failed to go by. If this sort of selectivity had been possible for Billy, he might have chosen as his happiest moment his sun-drenched snooze in the back of the wagon.

Billy Pilgrim was armed as he snoozed. It was the first time he had been armed since basic training. His compan-ions had insisted that he arm himself, since God only knew what sorts of killers might be in burrows on the face of the moon—wild dogs, packs of rats fattened on corpses, escaped maniacs and murderers, soldiers who would never quit killing until they themselves were killed.

Billy had a tremendous cavalry pistol in his belt. It was a relic of World War One. It had a ring in its butt. It was loaded with bullets the size of robins' eggs. Billy had found it in the bedside table in a house. That was one of the things about the end of the war: Absolutely anybody who wanted a weapon could have one. They were lying all around. Billy had a saber, too. It was a Luftwaffe ceremonial saber. Its hilt was stamped with a screaming eagle. The eagle was carrying a swastika and looking down. Billy found it stuck into a telephone pole. He had pulled it out of the pole as the wagon went by.

Now his snoozing became shallower as he heard a man and a woman speaking German in pitying tones. The speakers were commiserating with somebody lyrically. Before Billy opened his eyes, it seemed to him that the tones might have been those used by the friends of Jesus when they took His ruined body down from His cross. So it goes.

Billy opened his eyes. A middle-aged man and wife were crooning to the horses. They were noticing what the Americans had not noticed—that the horses' mouths were bleeding, gashed by the bits, that the horses' hooves were broken, so that every step meant agony, that the horses were insane with thirst. The Americans had treated their form of transportation as though it were no more sensitive than a six-cylinder Chevrolet.

These two horse pitiers moved back along the wagon to where they could gaze in patronizing reproach at Billy—at Billy Pilgrim, who was so long and weak, so ridiculous in his azure toga and silver shoes. They weren't afraid of him. They weren't afraid of anything. They were doctors, both obstetricians. They had been delivering babies until the hospitals were all burned down. Now they were picnicking near where their apartment used to be.

The woman was softly beautiful, translucent from having eaten potatoes for so long. The man wore a business suit, necktie and all. Potatoes had made him gaunt. He was as tall as Billy, wore steel-rimmed tri-focals. This couple, so involved with babies, had never reproduced themselves, though they could have. This was an interesting comment on the whole idea of reproduction.

They had nine languages between them. They tried Polish on Billy Pilgrim first, since he was dressed so clownishly, since the wretched Poles were the involuntary clowns of the Second World War.

Billy asked them in English what it was they wanted, and they at once scolded him in English for the condition of the horses. They made Billy get out of the wagon and come look at the horses. When Billy saw the condition of his means of transportation, he burst into tears. He hadn't cried about anything else in the war.

Later on, as a middle-aged optometrist, he would weep quietly and privately sometimes, but never make loud *boohooing* noises.

Which is why the epigraph of this book is the quatrain from the famous Christmas carol. Billy cried very little, though he often saw things worth crying about, and in *that* respect, at least, he resembled the Christ of the carol:

> *The cattle are lowing,*
> *The Baby awakes.*
> *But the little Lord Jesus*
> *No crying He makes.*

Billy traveled in time back to the hospital in Vermont. Breakfast had been eaten and cleared away, and Professor Rumfoord was reluctantly becoming interested in Billy as a human being. Rumfoord questioned Billy gruffly, satisfied himself that Billy really had been in Dresden. He asked Billy what it had been like, and Billy told him about the horses and the couple picnicking on the moon.

The story ended this way: Billy and the doctors unharnessed the horses, but the horses wouldn't go anywhere. Their feet hurt too much. And then Russians came on motorcycles, and they arrested everybody but the horses.

Two days after that, Billy was turned over to the Americans, who shipped him home on a very slow freighter called the *Lucretia A. Mott*. Lucretia A. Mott was a famous American suffragette. She was dead. So it goes.

"It *had* to be done," Rumfoord told Billy, speaking of the destruction of Dresden.

"I know," said Billy.

"That's war."

"I know. I'm not complaining."

"It must have been hell on the ground."

"It was," said Billy Pilgrim.

"Pity the men who had to *do* it."

"I do."

"You must have had mixed feelings, there on the ground."

"It was all right," said Billy. *"Everything* is all right, and everybody has to do exactly what he does. I learned that on Tralfamadore."

Billy Pilgrim's daughter took him home later that day, put him to bed in his house, turned the Magic Fingers on. There was a practical nurse there. Billy wasn't supposed to work or even leave the house for a while, at least. He was under observation.

But Billy sneaked out while the nurse wasn't watching, and he drove to New York City, where he hoped to appear on television. He was going to tell the world about the lessons of Tralfamadore.

Billy Pilgrim checked into the Royalton Hotel on Forty-fourth Street in New York. He by chance was given a room which had once been the home of George Jean Nathan, the critic and editor. Nathan, according to the Earthling concept of time, had died back in 1958. According to the Tralfamadorian concept, of course, Nathan was still alive somewhere and always would be.

The room was small and simple, except that it was on the top floor, and had French doors which opened onto a terrace as large as the room. And beyond the parapet of the terrace was the air space over Forty-fourth Street. Billy now leaned over that parapet, looked down at all the people moving hither and yon. They were jerky little scissors. They were a lot of fun.

It was a chilly night, and Billy came indoors after a while, closed the French doors. Closing those doors reminded him of his honeymoon. There had been French doors on the Cape Ann love nest of his honeymoon, still were, always would be.

Billy turned on his television set, clicking its channel selector around and around. He was looking for programs on which he might be allowed to appear. But it was too early in the evening for programs that allowed people with peculiar opinions to speak out. It was only a little after eight o'clock, so all the shows were about silliness or murder. So it goes.

Billy left his room, went down the slow elevator, walked over to Times Square, looked into the window of a tawdry bookstore. In the window were hundreds of books about fucking and buggery and murder, and a street guide to New York City, and a model of the Statue of Liberty with a thermometer on it. Also in the window, speckled with soot and fly shit, were four paperback novels by Billy's friend, Kilgore Trout.

The news of the day, meanwhile, was being written in a ribbon of lights on a building to Billy's back. The window reflected the news. It was about power and sports and anger and death. So it goes.

Billy went into the bookstore.

A sign in there said that adults only were allowed in the back. There were peep shows in the back that showed movies of young women and men with no clothes on. It cost a quarter to look into a machine for one minute. There were still photographs of naked young people for sale back there, too. You could take those home. The stills were a lot more Tralfamadorian than the movies, since you could look at them whenever you wanted to, and they wouldn't change. Twenty years in the future, those girls would still be young, would still be smiling or smoldering or simply looking stupid, with their legs wide open. Some of them were eating lollipops or bananas. They would still be eating those. And the peckers of the young men would still be semierect, and their muscles would be bulging like cannonballs.

But Billy Pilgrim wasn't beguiled by the back of the store. He was thrilled by the Kilgore Trout novels in the front. The titles were all new to him, or he thought they were. Now he opened one. It seemed all right for him to do that. Everybody else in the store was pawing things. The name of the book was *The Big Board*. He got a few paragraphs into it, and then he realized that he *had* read it before—years ago, in the veterans' hospital. It was about an Earthling man and woman who were kidnapped by extra-terrestrials. They were put on display in a zoo on a planet called Zircon-212.

These fictitious people in the zoo had a big board supposedly showing stock market quotations and commodity prices along one wall of their habitat, and a news ticker, and a telephone that was supposedly connected to a brokerage on Earth. The creatures on Zircon-212 told their captives that they had invested a million dollars for them back on Earth, and that it was up to the captives to manage it so that they would be fabulously wealthy when they were returned to Earth.

The telephone and the big board and the ticker were all fakes, of course. They were simply stimulants to make the Earthlings perform vividly for the crowds at the zoo—to make them jump up and down and cheer, or gloat, or sulk, or tear their hair, to be scared shitless or to feel as contented as babies in their mothers' arms.

The Earthlings did very well on paper. That was part of the rigging, of course. And religion got mixed up in it, too. The news ticker reminded them that the President of the United States had declared National Prayer Week, and that everybody should pray. The Earthlings had had a bad week on the market before that. They had lost a small fortune in olive oil futures. So they gave praying a whirl.

It worked. Olive oil went up.

Another Kilgore Trout book there in the window was about a man who built a time machine so he could go back and see Jesus. It worked, and he saw Jesus when Jesus was only twelve years old. Jesus was learning the carpentry trade from his father.

Two Roman soldiers came into the shop with a mechanical drawing on papyrus of a device they wanted built by sunrise the next morning. It was a cross to be used in the execution of a rabble-rouser.

Jesus and his father built it. They were glad to have the work. And the rabble-rouser was executed on it.

So it goes.

The bookstore was run by seeming quintuplets, by five short, bald men chewing unlit cigars that were sopping wet. They never smiled, and each one had a stool to perch on. They were making money running a paper-and-celluloid whorehouse. They didn't have hard-ons. Neither did Billy Pilgrim. Everybody else did. It was a ridiculous store, all about love and babies.

The clerks occasionally told somebody to buy or get out, not to just look and look and look and paw and paw. Some of the people were looking at each other instead of the merchandise.

A clerk came up to Billy and told him the good stuff was in the back, that the books Billy was reading were window dressing. "That ain't what you want, for Christ's sake," he told Billy. "What you want's in *back*."

So Billy moved a little farther back, but not as far as the part for adults only. He moved because of absentminded politeness, taking a Trout book with him—the one about Jesus and the time machine.

The time-traveler in the book went back to *Bible* times to find out one thing in particular: Whether or not Jesus had really died on the cross, or whether he had been taken down while still alive, whether he had really gone on living. The hero had a stethoscope along.

Billy skipped to the end of the book, where the hero mingled with the people who were taking Jesus down from the cross. The time-traveler was the first one up the ladder, dressed in clothes of the period, and he leaned close to Jesus so people couldn't see him use the stethoscope, and he listened.

There wasn't a sound inside the emaciated chest cavity. The Son of God was dead as a doornail.

So it goes.

The time-traveler, whose name was Lance Corwin, also got to measure the length of Jesus, but not to weigh him. Jesus was five feet and three and a half inches long.

Another clerk came up to Billy and asked him if he was going to buy the book or not, and Billy said that he wanted to buy it, please. He had his back to a rack of paperback books about oral-genital contacts from ancient Egypt to the present and so on, and the clerk supposed Billy was reading one of these. So he was startled when he saw what Billy's book was. He said, "Jesus Christ, where did you find this thing?" and so on, and he had to tell the other clerks about the pervert who wanted to buy the window dressing. The other clerks already knew about Billy. They had been watching him, too.

The cash register where Billy waited for his change was near a bin of old girly magazines. Billy looked at one out of the corner of his eye, and he saw this question on its cover: *What really became of Montana Wildhack?*

So Billy read it. He knew where Montana Wildhack *really* was, of course. She was back on Tralfamadore, taking care of the baby, but the magazine, which was called *Midnight Pussycats,* promised that she was wearing a cement overcoat under thirty fathoms of saltwater in San Pedro Bay.

So it goes.

Billy wanted to laugh. The magazine, which was published for lonesome men to jerk off to, ran the story so it could print pictures taken from blue movies which Montana had made as a teen-ager. Billy did not look closely at these. They were grainy things, soot and chalk. They could have been anybody.

Billy was again directed to the back of the store, and he went this time. A jaded sailor stepped away from a movie machine while the film was still running. Billy looked in, and there was Montana Wildhack alone on a bed, peeling a banana. The picture clicked off. Billy did not want to see what happened next, and a clerk importuned him to come over and see some really hot stuff they kept under the counter for connoisseurs.

Billy was mildly curious as to what could possibly have been kept hidden in such a place. The clerk leered and showed him. It was a photograph of a woman and a Shetland pony. They were attempting to have sexual intercourse between two Doric columns, in front of velvet draperies which were fringed with deedlee-balls.

Billy didn't get onto television in New York that night, but he *did* get onto a radio talk show. There was a radio station right next to Billy's hotel. He saw its call letters over the entrance of an office building, so he went in. He went up to the studio on an automatic elevator, and there were other people up there, waiting to go in. They were literary critics, and they thought Billy was one, too. They were going to discuss whether the novel was dead or not. So it goes.

Billy took his seat with the others around a golden oak table, with a microphone all his own. The master of ceremonies asked him his name and what paper he was from. Billy said he was from the *Ilium Gazette*.

He was nervous and happy. "If you're ever in Cody, Wyoming," he told himself, "just ask for Wild Bob."

Billy put his hand up at the very first part of the program, but he wasn't called on right away. Others got in ahead of him. One of them said that it would be a nice time to bury the novel, now that a Virginian, one hundred years after Appomattox, had written *Uncle Tom's Cabin*. Another one said that people couldn't read well enough anymore to turn print into exciting situations in their skulls, so that authors had to do what Norman Mailer did, which was to perform in public what he had written. The master of ceremonies asked people to say what they thought the function of the novel might be in modern society, and one critic said, "To provide touches of color in rooms with all-white walls." Another one said, "To describe blow-jobs artistically." Another one said, "To teach wives of junior executives what to buy next and how to act in a French restaurant."

And then Billy was allowed to speak. Off he went, in that beautifully trained voice of his, telling about the flying saucers and Montana Wildhack and so on.

He was gently expelled from the studio during a commercial. He went back to his hotel room, put a quarter into the Magic Fingers machine connected to his bed, and he went to sleep. He traveled in time back to Tralfamadore.

"Time-traveling again?" said Montana. It was artificial evening in the dome. She was breast-feeding their child.

"Hmm?" said Billy.

"You've been time-traveling again. I can always tell."

"Um."

"Where did you go this time? It wasn't the war. I can tell that, too."

"New York."

"The Big Apple."

"Hm?"

"That's what they used to call New York."

"Oh."

"You see any plays or movies?"

"No—I walked around Times Square some, bought a book by Kilgore Trout."

"Lucky *you*." She did not share his enthusiasm for Kilgore Trout.

Billy mentioned casually that he had seen part of a blue movie she had made. Her response was no less casual. It was Tralfamadorian and guilt-free:

"Yes—" she said, "and I've heard about you in the war, about what a clown you were. And I've heard about the high-school teacher who was shot. He made a blue movie with a firing squad." She moved the baby from one breast to the other, because the moment was so structured that she *had* to do so.

There was a silence.

"They're playing with the clocks again," said Montana, rising, preparing to put the baby into its crib. She meant that their keepers were making the electric clocks in the dome go fast, then slow, then fast again, and watching the little Earthling family through peepholes.

There was a silver chain around Montana Wildhack's neck. Hanging from it, between her breasts, was a locket containing a photograph of her alcoholic mother—a grainy thing, soot and chalk. It could have been anybody. Engraved on the outside of the locket were these words:

God grant me the serenity to accept the things I cannot change, courage to change the things I can, and wisdom always to tell the difference

≡ 10 ≡

Robert Kennedy, whose summer home is eight miles from the home I live in all year round, was shot two nights ago. He died last night. So it goes.

Martin Luther King was shot a month ago. He died, too. So it goes.

And every day my Government gives me a count of corpses created by military science in Vietnam. So it goes.

My father died many years ago now—of natural causes. So it goes. He was a sweet man. He was a gun nut, too. He left me his guns. They rust.

On Tralfamadore, says Billy Pilgrim, there isn't much interest in Jesus Christ. The Earthling figure who is most engaging to the Tralfamadorian mind, he says, is Charles Darwin—who taught that those who die are meant to die, that corpses are improvements. So it goes.

The same general idea appears in *The Big Board* by Kilgore Trout. The flying saucer creatures who capture Trout's hero ask him about Darwin. They also ask him about golf.

If what Billy Pilgrim learned from the Tralfamadorians is true, that we will all live forever, no matter how dead we may sometimes seem to be, I am not overjoyed. Still—if I am going to spend eternity visiting this moment and that, I'm grateful that so many of those moments are nice.

One of the nicest ones in recent times was on my trip back to Dresden with my old war buddy, O'Hare.

We took a Hungarian Airlines plane from East Berlin. The pilot had a handlebar mustache. He looked like Adolph Menjou. He smoked a Cuban cigar while the plane was being fueled. When we took off, there was no talk of fastening seat belts.

When we were up in the air, a young steward served us rye bread and salami and butter and cheese and white wine. The folding tray in front of me would not open out. The steward went into the cockpit for a tool, came back with a beer-can opener. He used it to pry out the tray.

There were only six other passengers. They spoke many languages. They were having nice times, too. East Germany was down below, and the lights were on. I imagined dropping bombs on those lights, those villages and cities and towns.

O'Hare and I had never expected to make any money—and here we were now, extremely well-to-do.

"If you're ever in Cody, Wyoming," I said to him lazily, "just ask for Wild Bob."

O'Hare had a little notebook with him, and printed in the back of it were postal rates and airline distances and the altitudes of famous mountains and other key facts about the world. He was looking up the population of Dresden, which wasn't in the notebook, when he came across this, which he gave me to read:

On an average, 324,000 new babies are born into the world every day. During that same day, 10,000 persons, on

*an average, will have starved to death or died from mal-
nutrition.* So it goes. *In addition, 123,000 persons will die
for other reasons.* So it goes. *This leaves a net gain of about
191,000 each day in the world. The Population Reference
Bureau predicts that the world's total population will
double to 7,000,000,000 before the year 2000.*

"I suppose they will all want dignity," I said.

"I suppose," said O'Hare.

Billy Pilgrim was meanwhile traveling back to Dresden,
too, but not in the present. He was going back there in
1945, two days after the city was destroyed. Now Billy and
the rest were being marched into the ruins by their guards.
I was there. O'Hare was there. We had spent the past two
nights in the blind innkeeper's stable. Authorities had
found us there. They told us what to do. We were to
borrow picks and shovels and crowbars and wheelbarrows
from our neighbors. We were to march with these imple-
ments to such and such a place in the ruins, ready to go to
work.

There were barricades on the main roads leading into
the ruins. Germans were stopped there. They were not
permitted to explore the moon.

Prisoners of war from many lands came together that
morning at such and such a place in Dresden. It had been
decreed that here was where the digging for bodies was to
begin. So the digging began.

Billy found himself paired as a digger with a Maori, who
had been captured at Tobruk. The Maori was chocolate
brown. He had whirlpools tattooed on his forehead and his
cheeks. Billy and the Maori dug into the inert, unpromis-

ing gravel of the moon. The materials were loose, so there were constant little avalanches.

Many holes were dug at once. Nobody knew yet what there was to find. Most holes came to nothing—to pavement, or to boulders so huge they would not move. There was no machinery. Not even horses or mules or oxen could cross the moonscape.

And Billy and the Maori and others helping them with their particular hole came at last to a membrane of timbers laced over rocks which had wedged together to form an accidental dome. They made a hole in the membrane. There was darkness and space under there.

A German soldier with a flashlight went down into the darkness, was gone a long time. When he finally came back, he told a superior on the rim of the hole that there were dozens of bodies down there. They were sitting on benches. They were unmarked.

So it goes.

The superior said that the opening in the membrane should be enlarged, and that a ladder should be put in the hole, so that the bodies could be carried out. Thus began the first corpse mine in Dresden.

There were hundreds of corpse mines operating by and by. They didn't smell bad at first, were wax museums. But then the bodies rotted and liquefied, and the stink was like roses and mustard gas.

So it goes.

The Maori Billy had worked with died of the dry heaves, after having been ordered to go down in that stink and work. He tore himself to pieces, throwing up and throwing up.

So it goes.

So a new technique was devised. Bodies weren't brought up any more. They were cremated by soldiers with flame-throwers right where they were. The soldiers stood outside the shelters, simply sent the fire in.

Somewhere in there the poor old high school teacher, Edgar Derby, was caught with a teapot he had taken from the catacombs. He was arrested for plundering. He was tried and shot.

So it goes.

And somewhere in there was springtime. The corpse mines were closed down. The soldiers all left to fight the Russians. In the suburbs, the women and children dug rifle pits. Billy and the rest of his group were locked up in the stable in the suburbs. And then, one morning, they got up to discover that the door was unlocked. World War Two in Europe was over.

Billy and the rest wandered out onto the shady street. The trees were leafing out. There was nothing going on out there, no traffic of any kind. There was only one vehicle, an abandoned wagon drawn by two horses. The wagon was green and coffin-shaped.

Birds were talking

One bird said to Billy Pilgrim, *"Poo-tee-weet?"*